'How are you going to search for Mrs Right?'

'I'll ask someone to help me,' J.D. said.

'Who?'

'You.'

Katie blinked owlishly, then leaned back in her chair as she narrowed her eyes to study him. 'Me?'

He drew a deep breath and forged ahead. 'Yeah. I'd like you to help me find a wife.'

D1343842

Dear Reader

After I introduced J. D. Berkley in FOR A CHILD'S SAKE, I decided that I couldn't let him fade into obscurity before he experienced his own happy ending. The *Bachelor Doctor* series became the perfect opportunity for the spotlight to shine on this die-hard bachelor.

As I pondered J.D.'s situation, I soon discovered that I couldn't ignore Katie Alexander either. She'd first appeared as a teenager in A FRESH DIAGNOSIS and later as a professional in FOR A CHILD'S SAKE. Since I wanted to continue the same 'friendship' theme as in my *Sisters at Heart* trilogy, I paired the two close acquaintances and had interesting results! HIS MADE-TO-ORDER BRIDE is their story.

I hope you enjoy sharing in the adventure. Happy Reading!

Jessica Matthews

Recent titles by the same author:

BABIES ON HER MIND
A HERO FOR MOMMY
DR PRESCOTT'S DILEMMA
A HEALING SEASON
TOO CLOSE FOR COMFORT*
HEART OF GOLD*
FOR A CHILD'S SAKE*
A FRESH DIAGNOSIS
THE CALL OF DUTY

* *Sisters at Heart* trilogy

HIS MADE-TO-ORDER BRIDE

BY

JESSICA MATTHEWS

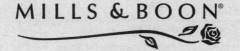

MILLS & BOON®

To my brother Steve, who brought a wonderful
woman into the family seventeen years ago.

DID YOU PURCHASE THIS BOOK WITHOUT A COVER?

If you did, you should be aware it is **stolen property** as it was reported
unsold and destroyed by a retailer. Neither the author nor the publisher
has received any payment for this book.

*All the characters in this book have no existence outside the imagination
of the author, and have no relation whatsoever to anyone bearing the
same name or names. They are not even distantly inspired by any
individual known or unknown to the author, and all the incidents are
pure invention.*

*All Rights Reserved including the right of reproduction in whole or in
part in any form. This edition is published by arrangement with
Harlequin Enterprises II B.V. The text of this publication or any part
thereof may not be reproduced or transmitted in any form or by any
means, electronic or mechanical, including photocopying, recording,
storage in an information retrieval system, or otherwise, without the
written permission of the publisher.*

*This book is sold subject to the condition that it shall not, by way of
trade or otherwise, be lent, resold, hired out or otherwise circulated
without the prior consent of the publisher in any form of binding or
cover other than that in which it is published and without a similar
condition including this condition being imposed on the subsequent
purchaser.*

*MILLS & BOON and MILLS & BOON with the Rose Device
are registered trademarks of the publisher.*

*First published in Great Britain 1999
Harlequin Mills & Boon Limited,
Eton House, 18-24 Paradise Road, Richmond, Surrey TW9 1SR*

© Jessica Matthews 1999

ISBN 0 263 81836 5

*Set in Times Roman 10½ on 12 pt.
03-9911-43405-D*

*Printed and bound in Spain
by Litografia Rosés S.A., Barcelona*

CHAPTER ONE

'IT'S time you were married, James.'

James Berkley, known as J.D. to his friends, stared at his mother in open-mouthed incredulity. 'You called me away from a patient to tell me *that*?'

At once he turned to frown at Katie Alexander, a former emergency medical technician and a recent nursing school graduate who'd summoned him with an urgent message from his mother. The apprehension on Katie's face as she'd poked her head into his cubicle had convinced him to come immediately.

Expecting the worst, he'd hurried to meet his mother. And for what? To hear her tell him to get married.

Katie, an average-sized brunette with a cheerful disposition, clearly disregarded his black look as she casually shrugged. 'Hey, don't blame me. She said it concerned Daniel and since your patient has to wait for X-rays I thought you'd want to hear what your mom had to say.'

He started to object again, but Virginia broke in. 'My conversation *does* concern Daniel. Indirectly.'

J.D. shot her one of his quelling glances, but Virginia, true to the backbone of steel underlying her southern gentility, didn't flinch under his intimidating gaze.

'I don't regret stretching the truth for the chance to see you before I left town,' she said in her slow

Texas drawl, 'so don't take your frustration out on the poor girl.'

Katie grinned. 'Yeah, *Doctor*. Listen to your mother.'

J.D. pinched the bridge of his nose. There were times when he wished his relationship with Katie wasn't so easy-going. She didn't cower under his sharp-eyed gaze like most of the nursing staff.

'As for myself,' Katie continued, 'I'm glad to hear that Daniel isn't sick. It's October and not uncommon for kids to catch a bug of one sort or another.'

'I agree, but the ER isn't the place for this particular discussion,' he stated firmly, silently warning Katie of the ramifications if she didn't keep Virginia's opening statement under wraps. Sheer luck had granted them privacy. He thanked whatever fates had been responsible for orchestrating the feat.

A bland expression crossed Katie's face before she turned aside to rummage through a drawer for a fresh ink pen. 'Don't mind me. I didn't hear a thing.'

'May I please continue?' Virginia interrupted. 'I've spent the last few days with you and Daniel and while I've held my peace during the entire time I won't any longer.'

'Look, Mom,' he said, allowing a note of desperation to colour his tone. 'Why don't we talk about this later?'

Virginia shook her head, without dislodging a single blonde hair of her short, sleek hairstyle. She was a petite woman who dressed impeccably, as befitting a woman of her social status. She'd come from a family who could trace their roots to the Mayflower and who had possessed the luck and foresight to invest in oil-rich land.

In spite of, or perhaps because of, her diminutive stature, she'd learned the fine art of command to get what she wanted. With several West Point and Annapolis graduates in her genealogy, her ability came naturally.

'I'm sorry, but this simply can't wait. The current state of affairs has gone on long enough. As you know, your father and I haven't interfered in your life these past four years.'

J.D. raised one eyebrow and she amended her statement. 'At least, not much. However I refuse to stand by and say nothing while my grandson's mental health is at stake.'

He gritted his teeth, once again thinking of the patients needing medical attention. He didn't have the time or the inclination to argue. 'Daniel is a healthy, *well-adjusted* child. You've said so, yourself.'

Expecting her to embark on a debate, he held up his hands to forestall it. 'In any case, you voiced your opinion. Now you can go home in good conscience.'

'I'm not leaving until you understand the seriousness of the situation.' Virginia crossed her arms, looking as if she intended to stay for the duration.

'Right now, I understand that I have patients waiting, Mother. You know, *sick* people?'

'I'm well aware of the demands of your job, J.D.,' Virginia said in her no-nonsense voice, her back ramrod stiff. 'If you'd quit wasting precious time, you could return to work.'

Katie closed the drawer and straightened. 'The

lounge is free,' she offered, obviously trying to be helpful.

'You'll miss your flight,' he said, ignoring Katie's suggestion.

'Then I'll catch a later one,' Virginia said, waving her manicured hand in careless abandon.

His temples began to throb and he recognised the beginnings of a tension headache. Nothing short of an act of God would divert his mother's attention until the bee in her bonnet had been shaken loose.

'Fine. Let's go to the lounge.'

Wasting no time, he strode toward the employees' private sanctuary, with Virginia following at his heels. He flung open the door and took a bracing breath, ignoring the odour of the baked cod someone had purchased from the hospital cafeteria.

She spoke as soon as he closed the door. 'You may not believe me when I say this, but Daniel needs a mother.'

J.D. poured the last dregs of coffee into his mug and flipped the unit's switch to 'off'. He didn't care if it was leaning towards being a solid rather than a liquid; he intended to fortify himself for an unpleasant conversation.

'What brought on this revelation?' he asked, hiding the fact that the same thoughts had run through his mind from time to time. However, he'd always dismissed them as easily as they'd come.

'Before I left Daniel at his pre-school we stopped at the market where I heard the most awful gossip.'

'That's your problem, Mom. You're listening to a bunch of old biddies who don't have anything to do all day but embellish the truth.'

'For your information, these weren't "old biddies'',' she replied tartly. 'They had young children with them. One woman even had an infant.'

He raised his mug in a salute. 'I stand corrected.'

'Regardless, you're getting quite a reputation.'

J.D.'s exasperation turned to amusement. 'I am?'

'Absolutely,' Virginia declared. 'Women are in and out of your house like it has a revolving door. Young, old and everyone in between. I don't need to describe in detail what everyone believes. "Kinky" was mentioned. So was "gay".'

He rolled his eyes in disgust. 'Oh for…' His voice died. 'Not true. Just because three or four women help with Daniel, that doesn't mean I'm having a relationship with them. And, since I'm not, it doesn't mean my sexual preferences are skewed.'

Virginia interrupted. 'No, but you know how people talk. Do you want Daniel exposed to rumour and innuendo? Children repeat their parents' conversations, you know.'

'My two neighbours are your age, Mom,' he reminded her. 'Both of them are dying for a grandchild to spoil, so they dote on Daniel. We have a wonderful arrangement—Martha cooks, Henrietta cleans and they take turns looking after Daniel in the mornings and bringing him to day care.

'Then Katie picks him up when she gets off at three and watches him until I come home later in the evening. When she's unavailable I call some other friends I know who are willing to look after him for a few hours. He's used to being around different people.'

'Aha!' Virginia stated triumphantly. 'Daniel doesn't know a stranger. Anyone could request to take him home and he'd willingly go with them.'

J.D. rubbed the back of his neck. 'We have safeguards in place, Mom. Not only do we have a schedule posted at home so he's aware of where he's going and with whom, but we've talked about strangers. And we have a password.'

'I'm sure you have all the bases covered, so to speak, but your son needs continuity in his life. He shouldn't be passed from caretaker to caretaker like an unwanted puppy. The poor child practically lives out of a suitcase.'

J.D. thought of Daniel's tote bag leaning against his closet door, waiting for someone to unpack the clothes and toys inside. He quickly squelched the guilt his mother's comments created.

'Daniel likes all of his sitters,' he stated firmly. 'This arrangement has worked well for everyone. But if it will make you happier, I'll advertise for a live-in nanny.'

'Daniel needs a mother, and *you*,' Virginia emphasised, 'need a wife. Please, don't take this wrong, but you're getting positively dull. The lively young man I raised has disappeared.'

He gave a small smile, remembering the escapades of his younger days. The demands of medical school had curbed some of his spirit, but not all of it. Everything had changed, however, when Ellen had disappeared from his life.

'He grew up, Mom.'

'Nonsense. Ellen's death was difficult for you, but after all this time you simply must close that chapter and begin a new one. It isn't healthy for you or for Daniel.'

'Mother—' he began.

'It's time you started looking for someone to

share your life,' Virginia continued, as if he hadn't tried to interrupt. 'One of these days Daniel will move away from home and you'll be left alone.'

'Daniel's four. I shouldn't need to worry about that happening soon,' he said dryly.

'Believe me, the years fly by. It was only yesterday when you were his age, asking the same one hundred and one questions he does.' Her eyes grew misty before she blinked the moisture away. 'Just look at you. Thirty-six years old and a doctor. It doesn't seem possible.'

He hated it when his mother turned sentimental. He could hold his own when it came to facts and logic, but when she became emotional he had no defence.

Virginia placed a hand over his. 'I want you to be happy, James.'

'I am.'

She didn't appear convinced. 'You always told me how much you hated being an only child. You informed me on several occasions that our house was a mausoleum in comparison to everyone else's.'

The memory brought a faint smile to his mouth. Returning from a visit with his friends, it had been like stepping into another world, one without the boisterous noise of family living. While his buddies had envied him not having pesky siblings underfoot, he'd anticipated sleepovers at their houses with the same eagerness as Christmas and birthdays.

Times were different, though. If things had worked out with Ellen, perhaps his childish dream would have come true. The proverbial lemons had rolled into his life and J.D. was doing his best to turn the sour fruit into lemonade.

'I'm not getting married just so Daniel will have a mother.' He spoke adamantly. 'If I could juggle my career with the demands of an infant, I certainly can manage my work with a pre-school child.'

'That's not the point. You both would benefit from having a feminine influence in your lives.'

'With all the women parading through my home, I thought I had plenty,' he said, tongue-in-cheek.

She narrowed her eyes in a glance intended to stifle his mocking tone. 'A *permanent* feminine influence. In any case, I'm only asking you to start making yourself available. Start checking out the single young ladies in town for suitability, then let them know you're ready for a relationship. You're a good catch, if I say so myself.'

'I'm not a fish and I'm not interested in being *caught*. When I run across the right person, I'll act on it. In the meantime—'

'If you think this so-called ''right'' person will fall from the sky and into your lap, you can think again,' Virginia said tartly. 'You have to put forward *some* effort.'

Obviously nothing he said would change her mind. If allowing her to believe that he was obeying her suggestion gave him a respite from her interference, he refused to feel remorse over the small deception.

'OK, OK. Point taken. I'll keep my eyes open for Mrs Right.' If the perfect woman crossed his path, well and good. If she didn't, so be it. He didn't intend to beat the bushes to find her.

A satisfied expression crossed Virginia's face. 'I'm glad you've seen the light.'

'Remember, though, Mercer is a small town,' he

cautioned, trying to squash any great expectations she might have. 'Eligible women are hard to come by.'

Virginia pursed her lips. 'I suppose so. In that case, I'll work on it from my end, too.' She tapped a forefinger to one temple. 'Moving to Mercer might be a drawback. You aren't interested in returning to the city, are you?'

'No, I'm not.'

'Hmm,' she said thoughtfully. 'The location might not pose an insurmountable problem. Mercer is a quaint community. A bit lacking in cultural opportunities, perhaps, but there are worse places to live. I'm sure I can find a charming young woman who sees the benefits of marriage to a handsome physician. The advantages will certainly outweigh any drawbacks to living in a small town.'

'I think I can handle this on my own,' he said dryly.

'I'm sure you can, but a little help wouldn't hurt.' She glanced at her watch. 'Oh, dear. Look at the time. I must be off. I'm so glad we had this chat and came to an understanding. Now, don't you feel better?'

He didn't, but refrained from comment.

Virginia gave him a hug which he genuinely reciprocated. 'I'll be in touch to check on your progress.' After issuing her parting statement, she glided out of the room.

Alone with his thoughts, J.D. stared at the swirls forming on top of his coffee. *Check on his progress?* Not likely! He didn't have the energy or interest to pursue a personal relationship at this stage of his life.

His first experience would have to suffice for the time being.

From the moment he'd seen Ellen McGraw, he'd gone positively nuts over her. He'd been filling in as a locum for his friend while he'd gone on his honeymoon. Ellen had been in town for a medical records convention, had developed a horrible case of laryngitis and dropped in for a prescription. During the course of the following weeks, he'd fallen hopelessly in love. Life simply couldn't have got any better, or so he'd thought.

His best-laid plans fell apart when he'd wanted to introduce her to his parents. Without warning, she'd sent him the proverbial 'Dear John' letter. Before he'd been able to convince her that her blue-collar background wouldn't matter to his blue-blooded family, she'd disappeared, lock, stock and barrel, from her apartment. No one had known a forwarding address, or if they had, they'd refused to divulge it.

During the subsequent months, he'd hired a private investigator, but leads had been non-existent. J.D. had secured a job in Mercer's ER and, by sheer luck, discovered that her trail had ended in the exact same place. Unfortunately, she'd been fatally injured in a car accident some months before his arrival. If not for the skill of Tristan Lockwood, her child— his son, Daniel—wouldn't have survived either.

His existence since then revolved around caring for the legacy Ellen had left behind and establishing his career. He had little time for anything else and truthfully, he liked it that way.

As for needing a wife, one certainly would have come in handy when Daniel had been an infant. He'd even contemplated entering into a marriage of convenience with Ellen's friend, Beth, but she'd been too much in love with Tristan to settle for second best.

In the end, he organised his life as best he could. A fair number of people criticised him for not allowing Beth and Tristan to adopt Daniel, as they'd planned before J.D. arrived on the scene. Katie, however, stepped in to help, without passing judgement and without offering unwelcome advice. She had been—and still was—a godsend.

His household arrangements had worked well since the day he'd brought Daniel home and consequently, he didn't intend to fix what wasn't broken. Yes, there were times when he felt like something in his life was missing—after Daniel had gone to bed and he was alone with his newspaper and the television remote—but that wasn't a good excuse to get married.

His mother would simply have to understand.

His resolve strengthened, he flung open the door and came face to face with Katie.

She visibly jumped, her brown eyes wide with surprise. 'Don't do that,' she scolded, tossing her nutmeg-colored ponytail over one shoulder. 'You scared the daylights out of me.'

'Who did you think would be in here?' he asked, amused by her reaction.

'I wasn't expecting to find you in the doorway,' she returned. 'No one has seen you since your mom left fifteen minutes ago. I assumed you were in here licking your wounds.'

'Hardly,' he said dryly. 'I've developed a tough enough shell that my mother can't inflict any damage.'

'Ah,' she said knowingly. 'Then you must have been fantasising over the future Mrs Doctor Berkley.'

'Regardless of what my mother believes, Daniel and I are doing just fine. I'll find the future Mrs Berkley when I'm good and ready. I won't be railroaded into marriage.'

Scepticism crossed her elfin features. 'Your mother sounded very serious. She won't let you off the hook.'

He groaned. 'Please. Mom has already referred to me as a good catch. I can't handle any more fishing references.'

'You don't want to hear about how there are lots of fish in the sea to choose from? Or how if you don't act, the one you want will get away? Then there's the one about catching as many as you can and throwing out the ones you don't want.'

'No, I don't.'

She snapped her fingers. 'Darn. In any case, Virginia's right. You're a very eligible bachelor in this community.'

'Yeah, well, eligible or not, I have patients to see.'

'Not any more. Marty took care of Mrs Natelson and her toe. You, on the other hand, have just received an important summons from Allan Yates. Delivered personally, I might add.'

His disposition improved instantly. 'Really? I'll bet it's over the proposal I gave him last week.'

'Probably so. Anyway…' she stepped forward to straighten the collar of his white lab coat '…he wants you there as soon as possible. Too bad you're not wearing a power suit today instead of scrubs.'

'I want to impress him with my proposal, not my appearance,' he commented, looking down on her from his six-foot height.

'I know, but it wouldn't hurt to look like the distinguished head of Mercer's Emergency Services that you are. Maybe you should change back into your street clothes.'

He shook his head. 'What he sees is what he gets. This distinguished head doesn't sit behind a desk all day.'

'Do you at least have a comb?'

He dug in his hip pocket and removed a small black plastic comb. Using his reflection in the window as a guide, he straightened his sandy-colored hair. 'Wish me luck.'

She displayed crossed fingers on both hands. 'You got it. Go and dazzle him with your statistics and your wit.'

'I'll do my best.'

Ten minutes later, as J.D. was seated across from Allan Yates in the chief CEO's office, he was once again reminded of why he hated hospital politics. He preferred sticking to what he knew best—medicine—and leaving the diplomacy and posturing to the statesmen.

However, as Katie had mentioned, his job as chief of Mercer Memorial's Emergency Services Department included those administrative duties he disliked. He had to play the politicking game—within reason—to get what he wanted.

Right now, he wanted to revamp his department to include the formation of a minor emergency centre—a place where the lesser emergencies could be treated without tying up rooms designed for more critical situations.

As he surveyed the professionally decorated room with its plush carpeting, hand-crafted bookcases and opulent furnishings, he refused to feel inadequate in his clean but comfortable scrubs. He led by action and example, not by decree, and he was proud of it.

Allan cleared his throat, clasped his hands together and placed them on top of his oak desk. 'You've prepared an impressive document, J.D.'

J.D. allowed himself a small smile, although inwardly he was grinning from ear to ear. After months of research, hours of organising facts and figures and a week of waiting for Yates's summons, the praise was like music to his ears.

'Thank you.'

'You realise, however, that another department has also requested the same area to expand their operation. My wife, Candace, has written a thorough proposal, too.'

J.D. didn't doubt his claim for one second. Candace Yates had had the good fortune to have her husband's insight in preparing her case.

'This puts me in quite a dilemma,' Allan continued. 'I usually give the board my recommendation—point out the pros and cons—but this time I'm between a rock and a hard place. I'd hate for someone to accuse me of showing favouritism.'

Although J.D. understood the man's quandary, he douted the sincerity of Allan's apologetic look. Allan was a personable man in his late forties who possessed a shrewd head for business, but whenever his termagant of a wife wanted something she was rumoured to make his life miserable until he granted her request.

Having seen Candace's *modus operandi* at first-hand, J.D. didn't discount the gossip. After seeing them together on one occasion, he'd been reminded of a nervous Yorkshire terrier yipping at the heels of a placid basset hound. For a fleeting moment, he wondered if anyone had ever summoned the nerve to call her Candy. If they had, he was sure the woman would have breathed fire on the hapless victim.

It was enough to make a man swear off the blessed state of matrimony.

'I understand your problem,' J.D. answered smoothly.

'As I'm sure you also know,' Allan said, 'that final decision rests with the hospital's board of directors.'

'Yes, I do.' Part of him sighed in relief that Allan didn't have the authority to kill his proposal before it received a proper hearing, otherwise, he doubted if an endorsement as high as the Presidential seal of approval would sway Allan's opinion in the Emergency Department's favor.

On the other hand, Mercer's BOD was a formidable bunch. At least three of its members weren't known to embrace change unless they didn't have any other viable options. Even so, he'd rather take his chances with them.

Allan leaned back in his chair, making the leather creak under his weight. 'Would you be interested in some constructive criticism?'

Suddenly wary of the administrator's motives,

J.D. nodded. He couldn't imagine what vital piece of information he had omitted from his report.

'The only problem I see with your proposal is…' He hesitated before he finished. 'Is you.'

CHAPTER TWO

J.D. HAD prepared himself to counter every possible argument, but Allan's personal attack left him momentarily speechless. 'Me?'

Allan nodded. 'A project of this magnitude requires commitment.'

J.D. forced himself to portray a calmness he didn't feel. 'I've been researching this idea for the past three months. This isn't something I dreamed up yesterday.'

'It's not the paperwork aspect. The board members might be more inclined to lend their approval if they're assured of your intentions to see the project to its completion.'

J.D. scoffed as he crossed his arms. 'Of course I'll see it through to the end. Why wouldn't I?'

'You don't have any long-lasting ties to our community.'

'I've lived and worked in Mercer for nearly four years,' J.D. pointed out. 'I've enjoyed living here and don't have any plans to hunt for a new job.'

'I'm sure everyone will be relieved to hear that, but you're not married.'

J.D. narrowed his eyes. 'What bearing does my marital status have on improving our emergency service?'

Allan hesitated. 'May I be blunt?'

J.D. mentally braced himself. 'Yes.'

'We're all aware of your privileged background,'

Allan began. 'Living in Mercer, your prospects of finding someone with a similar social standing are slim to none. Since you'll want to avoid the same situation you found yourself in before...'

J.D. knew he was referring to his ill-fated romance with Ellen. His blood pressure rose.

Allan cleared his throat. 'I'm sure you'll choose more wisely next time. In any case, a woman used to the Dallas jet set won't be satisfied living in Mercer. You wouldn't be the first man forced to concede to his wife's wishes.'

'Aren't you jumping the gun a little? I don't have a wife, nor do I have one in mind. And, for the record,' J.D. said coldly, 'I don't intend to get involved with any woman who objects to the location or scope of my medical practice.'

Allan didn't appear convinced. 'Be that as it may, if memory serves, you don't own your home either.'

'So?' J.D. didn't soften the belligerent note in his voice. 'What's wrong with renting?'

'It could be construed as you having no intentions to remain in this community for long. People who own property won't pick up and move at the first sign of adversity.'

Had Allan forgotten that houses could be sold? J.D. clamped his jaws together to refrain from saying something he might regret later. Suddenly the motivation behind the administrator's comments became crystal clear.

'This is about Leland, isn't it?' Leland Purdy was a single physician who'd come to Mercer a year ago. An eloquent speaker with enough ideas to turn the world around, he hadn't stayed long enough to implement the very changes he'd spearheaded. In the meantime, the section heads who'd tried to accommodate his wishes were forced to deal with the chaos he'd left behind.

'No, but now that you mention Leland I'm sure his name will come up in the discussion.'

J.D. was willing to bet money on the identity of the 'someone' who would point out the similarities between Leland and himself. Allan would plant enough doubt in the board's collective mind to make J.D.'s proposal sound risky. In the end, Allan's long association with Mercer Memorial would be pointed out and Candace's request would seem the more sensible of the two.

He cut right to the chase. 'So, the bottom line is since I'm not a happily married man with a mortgage my chances of the board approving my proposal are slim to none.'

Allan raised both hands as if to placate him. 'Well, now, J.D. I won't presume to second-guess our hospital BOD. I'm simply pointing out the obvious. As they say, forewarned is forearmed.'

Anxious to leave before his temper exploded, J.D. rose. 'Absolutely.'

'I'll certainly put in a good word for your project, though. Don't you worry.'

'I'm glad to hear it.' J.D. wasted little time in reaching the exit and took extra care to avoid slamming the door behind him.

He bestowed a forced smile on Allan's secretary in the outer office, before heading toward familiar— and friendly—territory.

He burst through the pendulum-like double doors intent on finding Katie. Not only did she share his vision for establishing an area specifically for the minor emergencies, but she was the person both he and Daniel had come to rely on for the past four years. A quiet, dependable, level-headed young lady, she looked after Daniel almost as much as he did.

Best of all, she acted as his sounding board. If there had ever been a time when he'd needed her in that capacity, it was now. Luckily, he found her sitting at the nurses' station.

Katie glanced at him, the smile on her face dying to a frown. 'I don't need to ask how your meeting went.'

He glowered. 'No, you don't.'

'What did Allan think of your report?'

He didn't hide his disgust as he plunked himself on a vacant office chair. 'The report was fine. And, to quote Allan, "an impressive document".'

A tense moment passed before she prompted, 'But?'

'But I'm a risky element.'

She stared at him in open-mouthed disbelief. 'What?'

J.D. patiently explained. 'Allan questions whether I'll be here to see my project to completion.'

'Where did he get *that* idea?'

'From Leland.'

'Dr Purdy?' Incredulity crossed her face. 'What has he got to do with anything?'

J.D. shrugged. 'Leland left for greener pastures. Allan thinks I will, too.'

'But Dr Purdy always said Mercer was a stepping-stone to bigger and better things. He was quite vocal about it.'

'Yeah, well, since we're both tarred with the same

brush of bachelorhood, Allan figures I'm just as footloose and fancy-free.'

Katie crossed her arms and her brown eyes blazed with indignation. 'That's preposterous! You're a single parent with responsibilities, and Dr Purdy had none. I doubt if the man even knew what the inside of his apartment looked like. He went out with nearly every woman in the county.'

J.D. was well aware of the other man's habits. His colleague had tried to include him on some of his evenings around town, but J.D. had never taken him up on his offers. Curiosity prompted him to ask, 'You went on a date with him, too?'

She appeared affronted. 'I said *nearly* every woman. I wasn't his type. In any case, it's an insult for Allan to lump you in the same category as that *Romeo.*'

J.D. straightened a paperclip, then reshaped it into a square. 'I'll admit I wasn't flattered by the comparison. Renting my house is also a point against me. I could skip town at a moment's notice.'

Her expression became thoughtful. 'Owning property does imply a certain amount of stability. It's also a good long-term investment.'

'Yeah, I suppose,' he said, thinking of the inherent worries associated with such a major purchase. He hadn't avoided purchasing a house—it was just that he was satisfied with the one he had. Nor did he have any complaints against his landlord—if something needed to be fixed, Mr Hepplewhite took care of it almost immediately.

As an added bonus, the location of his home was within walking distance of the hospital and a neighbourhood elementary school. As far as J.D. was concerned, he had an ideal arrangement.

'Next you'll tell me that I need something along the lines of a five-acre estate.'

'At the very least,' she said, a teasing glint in her eyes. 'You could even add a few horses, a couple of cows, a dog and a family of cats, too. My neighbour has a few kittens ready to wean. Daniel would love taking care of a kitty or two.'

'A dog, maybe. A cat? Forget it.'

She chuckled. 'Rambunctious little boys and playful puppies go together better than little boys and cats, I guess.'

Her smile died and her voice became tentative. 'What *are* you planning to do?'

An unholy thought occurred to him. 'Other than perform a sigmoidoscopy on Allan without anaesthetic?'

Her grin returned. 'Yeah. Other than that.'

'I'm willing to do what I can to improve the emergency services department. I'll buy a house, or build one if need be, but getting married is out of the question.'

Katie turned away to rummage through a drawer. 'You're right. That would be the ultimate sacrifice.'

Oddly enough, her voice sounded cool.

'You've always been honest with me,' he began, fearing he'd offended her in some way. 'Surely you can see my point. My proposal should stand on its own merits and nothing else.'

She straightened to meet his gaze. 'I won't argue with you. However, a few of the more conservative members may agree with Allan. You should be prepared for that eventuality.'

'The board is composed of intelligent people,' J.D. said. 'They'll see how much more efficient and cost-effective the ER will be if they approve my idea.'

'Are you willing to gamble that your personal life won't influence their decision?'

Part of him was, but a small voice warned him of the perils associated with assuming how people would think. Perhaps it wouldn't hurt if he conducted a little PR of his own before his report appeared on the next board meeting's agenda.

The first phase of his plan included paying a visit to Dr Robert Casey, the medical director. Unfortunately, J.D.'s medical skills were constantly called for as the day unfolded and he shelved his idea for the time being.

Around three o'clock, Katie caught him in the hallway before he could see his next patient and handed him a packet of radiology films. 'After you're through looking at these, I have two more kids with high temps and sore throats waiting. Can I put them in one of the trauma rooms?'

He hated the idea of tying up their triage facilities in case a life-threatening situation arrived, yet he couldn't accept making sick people wait unnecessarily.

In the end, he decided to play the odds. 'OK, but keep one available in case we get an ambulance call. Maybe I should give Yates a call so he can actually see what we deal with on a daily basis.'

'Good idea, but he plays golf on Wednesday afternoons. You'll have to catch him tomorrow.'

'It figures. Must be nice to take off whenever you want.'

'I'd settle for the opportunity to leave when my eight-hour shift is over.' With that parting statement, she disappeared.

Carrying the X-rays, J.D. strode into the cubicle where fifteen-year-old Alyssa Ford, still cradling her bandaged left hand in her lap, was waiting with her mother.

'Let's see what the pictures show,' he said as he thrust the films into the wall-mounted viewbox. He studied them for a few minutes, then gave his diagnosis.

'Your wrist is sprained, but not broken,' he informed the teenager. 'No volleyball for several weeks, I'm afraid.'

'But the season ends next week,' the girl protested. 'It doesn't feel bad if it's wrapped. Can't I play in the last game? I'm going to be one of the starters.'

He shook his head. 'I know it's tough to be on the injured list, but if you don't take care of yourself now you could do irreparable damage. Unless, of course, you don't ever want to play volleyball again?' He raised one eyebrow.

The girl's Cupid's-bow mouth formed a resigned pout. 'All right. If I have to sit out, I will.'

'Check with your family physician in a few weeks to get your medical release in case you want to participate in other sports. Any questions?'

The Fords' negative responses came simultaneously.

He gave Alyssa a sympathetic glance. 'It won't be for ever. If you play your cards right, there might be some young man who's interested in carrying your book bag for a while.'

Alyssa's eyes brightened and her cheeks turned pink as she obviously considered the possibilities.

Glad to see the teenager's spirits had lifted, he said his goodbyes, then left. Before he reached the nurses' station, Dr Casey intercepted him.

'J.D. I'm glad to have caught you. Can you spare a few minutes?' The slim, fifty-year-old chief of staff delivered his question in such a way that J.D. didn't dare refuse.

'Sure. I wanted to talk to you, anyway.' J.D. thrust his hospital-issue pen into the left breast pocket of his green scrub shirt, tucked the medical record under his arm and waited expectantly for his superior to speak first.

Dr Casey motioned towards the ambulance dock. 'Do you mind if we step outside? I'd rather get away from listening ears.'

Puzzled over the request, J.D. glanced at Katie who was standing behind the desk. Her wide eyes and the shrug of her shoulders suggested she knew as much as he did, which amounted to nothing.

He placed the Ford girl's chart on the counter. 'Fine with me. I could use a breath of fresh air.'

He strode alongside the other physician, comparing his shapeless scrubs to Robert's expertly tailored herringbone tweed suit, grey shirt and multicoloured silk tie. Funny thing how ever since Katie had made the comment about power suits, he'd become keenly conscious of his colleagues' attire.

His own closet was filled with similar apparel, but he had little occasion to wear them. Then again, he didn't feel the need or have the desire to impress people. In an emergency, no one cared what he wore; it was his expertise that counted.

The cool October breeze, the fresh scent of wood smoke from someone's fireplace and the open space was the perfect tonic to counteract the stuffy, crowded, sterile confines of the ER.

Taking a deep breath, he motioned Robert to a sheltered alcove. A sand-filled urn bearing a multitude of cigarette butts provided evidence of this being a popular spot among the smoking members of Mercer's staff.

'I'll get right to the point,' Robert said once they were alone. 'What's this I hear about you leaving town?'

J.D. walked into his kitchen later that evening and heard the soft whirl of Katie's sewing machine. Out of habit, he hung the keys to his van on the ornamental key hook near the door.

The dish of pepper steak and rice waiting in the refrigerator didn't appeal to him. Mentally exhausted from the day, even his favourite dessert of cherry cheesecake didn't tempt his taste buds. Considering the mood he was in, he needed something with a little more pizzazz to raise his spirits.

A six-pack of Coors beer—left over from a September Labour Day party—beckoned and he gratefully retrieved one bottle. He turned away from the fridge to screw off the cap and noticed Katie, standing in the doorway.

She wore a pair of blue denim jeans and an oversized red Kansas City Chiefs sweatshirt. The ends of her long light brown hair brushed against the bend of her elbow as she carried a wad of multicoloured fabric in her arms.

'It's ten o'clock. You're later than I'd expected,' she mentioned.

Her tentative tone reminded him of how short-tempered he'd been ever since his meeting with Robert. Even Katie had felt his bite and had wisely left him alone to the point where she didn't even say goodbye at the end of her shift as was her custom.

'Busy evening.' He took another long swig.

'Daniel's asleep.'

'I assumed he was.'

She held up the mass of material. 'I've been working on his Hallowe'en costume.'

'So he's finally decided on what he wants to be?'

Katie nodded. 'After watching Peter Pan, he chose Captain Hook. We found a package of props and some face paint at the store tonight. I hope you don't mind that I already bought them, but as it was the last set, I was afraid to wait.'

'Good idea.'

'Have you eaten?'

'Not since lunch.'

'Maybe you should.'

He caught her eyeing the nearly empty bottle in his hand. 'Don't worry, I will.'

'Want to talk about whatever's bothering you?'

J.D. sank onto a kitchen chair. 'Not really, but you may as well know the latest. In fact, I'm surprised you don't already know.'

She sat across from him. 'Sorry. I don't take time to gossip at work. Too busy.'

'Allan's started the rumour that I'm leaving Mercer.'

Her brown eyes widened. 'You're kidding. Are you sure?'

'I don't know it for a fact, but the odds of Allan being responsible are extremely good,' he said glumly, before polishing off the contents of his bottle. 'Dr Casey came specifically to the ER to ask if the story was true.'

She placed the half-finished costume on the table. 'So you set him straight. No big deal.'

'Ah, but, dear Katie, it *is* a big deal.' He rose to retrieve another bottle from the refrigerator. 'With the gossip floating around, Robert is afraid that my chances of the MEC getting approval are slim to none.'

'I don't see why,' she zealously defended him. 'Once you explain, the board will understand.'

'Ah, but therein lies the rub. I have to put my money where my mouth is. If I'm staying, which I am, then my actions have to corroborate my story.'

'Fine. Contact a Realtor and start looking for a house.'

'It's not quite so simple. To muddy the waters even more, two of the board members—Robert wouldn't name them, but I have a good idea who they are—don't hold too high an opinion of me. According to them, a single man has no business raising a child by himself when a couple was ready, willing and able.'

'They're still harping over ancient history? My word, that was four years ago!'

'Yeah, well, from their attitude, you'd think it happened yesterday.'

J.D. knew the Lockwoods would have cherished Daniel; they treated him as tenderly as one of their own now. In fact, if anything happened to him, he wouldn't object to them taking Daniel into their home.

The depth of Beth's and Tristan's love hadn't had any bearing on J.D.'s long-ago decision to assume responsibility for his son, however. It had boiled down to his need to look after the precious gift Ellen had left behind.

Apparently the self-righteous busybodies of Mercer couldn't understand such a novel concept.

On the flip side, those same critics would have found fault if he *hadn't* taken on his familial responsibilities. It was a definite no-win situation.

Disapproval over his decision had come from every side, but Katie had been a staunch supporter. He wouldn't have survived those dark days if not for her encouragement and her help.

'They're certainly not going to look favourably on any project I'll introduce,' he added.

Katie's eyes burned with a fierce light. 'Ophelia Weatherbee and Silas Cunningham, I'll bet. They should have retired from the board years ago. The sanctimonious pair of buzzards.'

He grinned at her apt description. 'Be that as it may, with their jaded opinion of me, plus Allan's behind-the-scenes manipulation, I only have one way to prove the gossip false.'

'From the way you're drowning your sorrows...' she motioned toward his bottle once again '...I assume your idea is more drastic than buying your own home.'

J.D. paused long enough for another swig. 'It is. I'm going to get married.'

'Married?' She sounded incredulous.

'It's crazy, I know.'

'But I thought you didn't want to.'

'I'm not averse to the institution of matrimony. I just haven't met the right person,' he clarified.

Katie pressed her lips together as she studied her fingernails for a long moment. 'Well, then. There's no need to ask who the lucky woman is.'

'Not yet.'

'Going to run an ad in the personal column?' she asked dryly. 'That should bring every single woman in Mercer knocking on your door.'

'Nope,' he said, wrapping his hands around the bottle. 'No personal ad. Like you said, since I'm such an eligible bachelor and a great catch, I'll have females crawling out of the woodwork.'

The smooth brown glass felt cool against his sweaty palms. Katie was vital to the success of his plan and if he couldn't convince her he was doomed.

'Then how are you going to search for Mrs Right?'

He clutched the bottle tightly. 'I'll ask someone to help me.'

'Who?'

'You.'

She blinked owlishly, then leaned back in her chair as she narrowed her eyes to study him. 'Me?'

He drew a deep breath and forged ahead. 'Yeah. I'd like you to help me find a wife.'

CHAPTER THREE

THE silence between them lengthened. J.D. held his breath, waiting and watching for Katie's response.

She rose in disgust. 'You're drunk.'

He was affronted. 'Not a chance. I'm only on my second beer.'

'Well, something has interfered with your thinking process,' she snapped. 'I'm going home.'

He jumped up to grab her elbow. 'You're the logical choice. It makes perfect sense.'

Her eyes shot sparks. 'To you, maybe. To me? Not a chance. I'm not running a dating service and I don't intend to start one either.'

'Will you hear me out?' He hesitated. 'Please?'

A mulish look appeared on her face, but she finally acquiesced. She sat, folding her arms across her chest.

'I'll listen to your nonsense for three minutes. Your hare-brained idea doesn't deserve that long, mind you, so start talking.'

J.D. pulled a chair away from the table, turned it around and sat down. He flashed her his most appealing smile, but her stiff countenance remained unchanged. This was going to be harder than he'd thought.

'You helped me find Martha and Henrietta.'

'Interviewing a housekeeper is different to scouting out prospective wives.'

He ignored her sarcasm. 'The point is, you know

35

both Daniel's and my tastes and our personalities. All I want is for you to recommend a few women and if necessary, make a few introductions. Consider yourself in an advisory capacity, screening the candidates, if you will.'

'Screen them yourself,' she said pertly. 'Or ask one of your friends for advice, like Tristan. I'm sure you'd rather have a male perspective anyway.'

He shook his head. 'Tristan and Beth won't be back for another month. Even if they hadn't left on their extended but well-deserved vacation, I trust your opinion and your instincts.'

'What's wrong with *your* instincts?'

'Nothing, but women are often more intuitive than men. You also know me better than anyone in Mercer.'

Katie toyed with the ends of her hair and looked thoughtful, but didn't reply.

'I want to do this discreetly,' he continued, leaning forward. 'I know what it's like to be chased and believe me when I say it's not an experience I want to repeat.'

He recalled one woman he'd gone out with BE— before Ellen—who'd convinced his apartment manager that she was a relative. He'd come home to find her preparing a Polynesian dish and wearing nothing but a lei and a grass skirt minus ninety-five per cent of the grass.

'Ask your mother for help. She'd be delighted.'

'I'd rather do it myself.'

'See?' she said brightly. 'You just admitted you'd rather find a wife yourself.' She started to rise and he grabbed her wrist with lightning speed.

'Please?' he asked, using his most cajoling tone.

'No.'

'Why not?'

'Why should I?' she countered.

'You'd have your life back.'

He watched her stiffen and her tone became brittle. 'What do you mean by that?'

'You've helped me from day one with whatever I needed and given up a good share of your life, caring for Daniel. To my regret, we haven't had an equitable arrangement. The list of what you've done for us is endless. Daniel and I have taken more from you than we've given in return.'

She squared her shoulders and her eyes burned brightly. 'For your information, J.D., I haven't done anything that I didn't *want* to do.'

'I know, but I can't help feeling that we're—that *I'm*—taking advantage of your generosity. When I consider how hard you worked for your nursing degree and still looked after Daniel…'

'Don't forget how you helped me study,' she reminded him.

'Yes, but wouldn't it have been easier if you had let us fend for ourselves?'

She fell silent and he pressed on. 'At least think about what I've asked. Give me your answer tomorrow.'

'I won't change my mind.'

He played his trump card. 'If I didn't have to worry about Daniel, I wouldn't ask for your help. Being a woman, you can sense who'd make a good mother.'

Pain flitted across her features and he quickly tamped down the shafts of guilt spearing his heart at causing her distress. Desperate times, however, required desperate measures.

She tugged her hand free. 'It's late and I want to go home.'

Afraid he'd already pushed her too hard, he nodded. 'I'll talk to you tomorrow.'

She didn't reply and he followed her into the tiny living room. He started to help her with her coat, but she stepped out of reach to avoid his touch. The deep hurt on her face struck at his heart, but he didn't understand her reaction to his request. He'd expected her to be flattered to be included in such a monumental decision. As he'd said, once he was married, she'd be free to do whatever she wanted.

'Goodnight,' he said as she opened the door and stepped into the night.

''Night.' The one word sounded husky in her throat.

He waited at the door until she'd started her car, turned on the headlights and pulled away from the kerb. His request had shocked her, that much was obvious, but Katie was level-headed and would see the rightness of it all.

Over the past four years, he couldn't remember her ever going out on a date. Katie's personal life had revolved around Daniel's needs and his schedule. If not for them, she could be nurturing a family and children of her own by now.

Truthfully, the idea of marriage was starting to grow on him. He wouldn't mind having someone around for companionship after Daniel had gone to bed; he wouldn't mind coming home to someone who greeted him as enthusiastically as Daniel did.

J.D. turned on the hallway light so he could peek

into his son's room without awakening him. He smiled at the sight of Daniel sprawled out in careless abandon, wearing the flannel baseball-print pyjamas Katie had made. The plastic toy hook dangled from the fingers of one hand, as if he'd hated to let his newest possession out of reach. J.D. had a feeling that it would be well used before the time came for it to be a part of Daniel's costume.

He crept quietly toward the bed and covered the child with his racing-car blanket. As he turned to leave, his gaze landed on the jumble of possessions covering the top of the dresser. One made him smile.

It was an oak leaf the size of a man's hand—the same one that had tumbled across J.D.'s path as he'd stood outside the ER, catching a breath of fresh air one day. Because its reddish-gold hue had matched the colour of Daniel's hair, he'd brought it home.

Thrilled with the unexpected gift, Daniel had deemed it worthy to place on his dresser along with his other treasures—a seashell, a rock dotted with flecks of fool's gold, a nail bent in the shape of a horseshoe and a framed snapshot of Ellen.

While Daniel bore a resemblance to his mother, he definitely was J.D.'s child. Daniel's photos matched those taken of J.D. at the same age, even down to his hazel eye colour. Daniel could look forward to having a squared jawline and patrician features in adulthood.

Ellen's picture tickled his memory and Daniel's often-voiced request for a mother echoed out as clearly as if Daniel had spoken them aloud.

J.D. squared his shoulders. With luck, and Katie's help, things would soon be different. It was time to exchange the Berkley *bachelor* household for the Berkley *family* home.

J.D. arrived at the work the next morning, wondering if he'd irrevocably damaged his friendship with Katie. As he strode into the ER, she greeted him politely but without her customary cheerfulness. Her dark eyes seemed tired and less animated. Now obviously wasn't the time to press for her decision.

'How's it going so far?' he asked, keeping the conversation work-related.

'Not bad. It's quiet right now. There's a pot of coffee on the burner, so you'd better grab some before it disappears.'

He sniffed the air. There was nothing like the smell of freshly brewed Colombian blend to start the day right. Scanning the duty board for today's assignments, he leaned closer to ask in a whisper, 'Who made it?'

'Don't you want to be surprised?'

He grimaced. 'My cast-iron stomach can only take so much. Only you and Beth make decent coffee. Since she's gone, I have to wait for you to fix it.'

'I don't suppose you've ever considered learning how to do it yourself? It isn't brain surgery, you know. I'd hate for you to be dependent on me.'

He winced at her coolly issued barb, knowing he deserved it.

'If you must know,' she said crossly, 'I made this pot.'

'Good,' he said, reaching inside the cupboard for the mug he'd received from a pharmaceutical rep promoting Viagra, the latest and greatest male potency pill. Eyeing the plate of cookies on the counter, he asked, 'Who brought those?'

'Ashley.'

He studied them with suspicion. 'Is this one of her own concoctions?'

'Yes.'

'Then I'll pass.' Ashley liked to modify tried-and-true recipes in her attempt to create new taste treats. Her goodies were inedible a good percentage of the time.

Before he could ask the question burning inside him, Katie changed the subject. 'I'm going to run down to the nursing director's office while we're not busy. Ashley will be here to cover, but if something big comes in you can page me. I shouldn't be gone for too long.'

Normally she would have been more forthcoming about her plans, especially as he knew how much she dreaded visiting with Mrs Morgan, the director of nursing usually referred to as Old Battle Axe.

He settled into a chair behind the desk with the latest medical journal, hoping to read at least one article before someone required his expertise. Fifteen minutes later Katie's co-worker, Ashley Dahlquist, sank into a chair beside him.

Conscious of his new goal, he let his gaze travel over Ashley's left hand. It was bare.

He leaned back to study her without her knowledge. She was pleasant-looking, had a nice figure and, from her conversations, liked to play racquetball. She'd graduated from this past year's nursing class along with Katie, but at twenty-seven Katie was a few years older and her years of service as an emergency medical technician had given her a confidence that Ashley lacked.

On the other hand, Ashley was congenial and anxious to please. Not bad wifely attributes, he thought, even if she couldn't cook. Before he could dwell further on the subject, Katie breezed through the double doors.

'I'm back.' Suddenly, she stopped short, her eyes wide with surprise. J.D. felt as if she knew that he'd looked at Ashley as a prospective marriage candidate rather than as another nurse. Her shoulders seemed to droop, along with the corners of her mouth.

'All clear here,' he said in an overly bright voice. ''Not a creature is stirring…'''

Ashley rose. 'We're getting low on syringes and gloves. Katie, do you think I should run to Central Supply and get a few more boxes?'

'Yeah. Good idea.'

Ashley left, intent on her task and apparently oblivious to the undercurrents flowing through the room.

Katie reached over the counter and pulled out the latest infection control policy from the slot designated for new policies. She spoke, avoiding his gaze.

'She's hoping to get an engagement ring this Christmas. Just thought you'd want to know.'

'I do.' He lowered his voice. 'Now do you see why I need your help?'

Her mouth formed a hard line and her nod seemed half-hearted. 'All right, but I have conditions.'

'Name them.'

She shook her head. 'We can discuss them later.'

'Tonight?' he asked hopefully. Now that he'd

committed himself to his course, he wanted to get started.

'OK. After Daniel's in bed.'

'Good idea.' The less Daniel knew, the better. He would announce to anyone who would listen that his daddy was finding him a mother. J.D. didn't need the aggravation or the publicity caused by such news.

'Fine. By the way, I'm using some of my over-time this afternoon.'

'Anything special planned?' he asked.

'Just doing a few things I've been putting off,' she said noncommittally.

The automatic doors leading from the ambulance bay whooshed open and two officers in tan-colored uniforms accompanied an orange-clad prisoner in handcuffs. The fellow was big and burly and, in J.D's opinion, weighed more than both of his keepers combined. A makeshift bandage covered his forehead and he held a rag to his nose.

To J.D.'s surprise, two more guards followed them.

Obviously this prisoner was a high security risk. J.D. couldn't recall having seen a similar situation at Mercer before and he took a closer look.

The prisoner shuffled along and he held his left arm against his side.

The deputies didn't appear unscathed either. Their hair was tousled and several sported bruises on their cheek-bones. Their expressions were hard, their eyes intent.

A tall blond approached Katie, the grim set to his mouth softening as he addressed her. 'Hi, Katykins.'

'Hello yourself, Thad,' she responded, her cheeks

pink-tinged and her face wearing the first smile J.D. had seen all day. 'What can we do for you fellows?'

Thad motioned to the prisoner. 'Ernie Sheldon here decided he didn't like to stay in our accommodations. He raised a ruckus to try and escape. He's a little worse for wear.'

J.D. eyed the man whose eyes seemed to shoot daggers. If looks could have killed, everyone in the ER would be dead, especially his jailers.

Thad continued. 'He's been complaining about his ribs so we thought we'd better bring him in for you folks to check out.'

J.D. exchanged a glance with Katie, visually signalling to her that he would remain nearby. 'Put him in One,' he ordered, wanting him away from the other ER patients.

Katie ushered the group into the specified exam room as J.D. followed. Although the staff usually took care of the basics, before calling him into the room, he didn't intend to leave Katie alone, even if Mr Sheldon was surrounded by four armed members of law enforcement.

He was also curious about the man who so comfortably modified Katie's name.

'Have a seat, Mr Sheldon,' Katie told him, motioning to the bed.

Thad and one of his colleagues stationed themselves near the foot and head of the cot. As the room wasn't designed to accommodate a large group, two of the deputies remained outside in the hallway. They stood on either side of the doorway, their legs planted apart as if they were ready to spring into action at the first sign of trouble.

J.D. remained in the background while Katie recorded their patient's full name—Ernest T Sheldon, his date of birth—he was forty-two—and his address.

At this last question, the man snorted. 'Just put down County Jail. I expect I'll be there a while.'

'After this stunt, it'll be a long while,' Thad assured him.

Sheldon turned the air blue with his comments about his jailers' parentage.

Katie rummaged in a drawer and withdrew an old-style mercury thermometer. She immediately shoved it in Sheldon's mouth to cut off his diatribe in mid-curse.

The silence in the room seemed golden as Katie continued with the usual taking of vital signs. J.D. took advantage of the momentary quiet to pose a few questions. 'You mentioned ribs. Anything else, other than the obvious?'

He referred to the bloodied bandage around the man's shaved head and his swollen nose.

Thad shook his head. 'No.'

J.D. addressed his patient just as Katie removed the thermometer from his mouth. 'Your ribs are sore?'

'Yeah. It's hard to catch my breath. Those s.o.b.s…' Sheldon added several more colourful expletives to describe his captors '…beat the holy hell out of me.'

Sensing the fellow was about to embark on another long tirade, J.D. interrupted. 'Any history of asthma or other lung problems?'

Sheldon shook his head.

J.D. pulled his stethoscope out of his pocket, aware that the handcuffs made the removal of the patient's shirt impossible. He raised the hem of Sheldon's orange tunic and began his exam.

As he listened to the whoosh of air in and out of the man's lungs, his visual exam showed the start of purplish areas across Sheldon's chest. Cracked ribs were a possibility, along with internal bruising to his kidneys.

At the same time, J.D. noticed how the prisoner's forearms were decorated with tattoos of everything from a heart with JULIA written inside to a skull and crossbones. A thick scar ran along the length of his jaw. His hands were the size of small hams and several fingers were crooked, as if they'd been previously broken.

Sheldon obviously didn't lead a peaceful existence.

'What about your family? Parents, grandparents?'

'Don't rightly know. Didn't know my grandparents and my dad died when I was a young 'un.'

'How would you describe the pain?' J.D. asked. 'Is it sharp or dull?'

'Depends. It's dull and then once in a while I get a sharp one. Stabs me clear through.'

J.D. continued his questioning while Katie pumped up the blood-pressure cuff and took a reading. 'How is it now?'

Sheldon thought a moment as if to assess the severity. 'Sort of dull.'

'Any nausea or vomiting?'

He shook his head.

'BP is 140 over 80. Pulse is 75,' Katie said as she slung her stethoscope around her neck.

'Can we take off the handcuffs?' J.D. asked one of the guards.

Thad shook his head. 'Not unless it's absolutely necessary. Do the best you can.'

His unyielding tone told J.D. not to press the issue at this point.

'Should I call X-Ray?' she asked.

'And the lab,' he replied. Immediately, she left the room to make the phone calls.

'What sort of physical activity do you do?' J.D. asked, as he patiently listened to the steady thump of the man's heart.

'Lifting weights, basketball.' He shrugged. 'Whatever they let us do while we're in the slammer.'

Seeing the size of the man's beefy arms, J.D. wondered how many pounds Sheldon could bench press. While J.D. himself wasn't a laggard when it came to exercise, he certainly wouldn't want to meet up with this man in a dark alley. The sports he himself indulged in—baseball, basketball and an occasional game of flag football—were more for fun than an actual physical regimen. Even so, he played often enough to keep in shape.

J.D. turned his attention to Sheldon's face. He carefully removed the bandage and inspected the gash. 'You're going to need a few stitches,' he commented. 'If we just put a butterfly on it, it won't heal as nicely.'

Sheldon's grin revealed tobacco-stained teeth. 'What's one more scar? But since the county's goin' to be footin' the bill, sew in as many as you want. That'll teach these idiots not to screw with me.'

J.D. sincerely doubted it. Considering Sheldon's size, sheer force would have been the only way to bring him down if he'd been trying to escape.

Katie strode in just as Sheldon embarked on another round of obscenities.

J.D. interrupted. 'I'm going to stitch up your head after we get blood and urine samples. We're also going to run a few X-rays and see if you've broken anything.'

'Hell, Doc. I didn't break a thing.' Sheldon motioned to Thad. 'It was our wonder boys here who done it.' He launched into his usual routine.

Katie placed the urine collection cup on the bed beside him. 'We need a sample.'

Sheldon eyed the plastic container. 'Now, honey, I ain't drank that much water. If you give me a few beers, well, then, I can oblige.'

'Do your best,' she ordered. 'The restroom's around the corner. I'll be back in a few minutes.'

The two deputies accompanied Sheldon while J.D. returned to the nurses' station with Katie.

J.D. scribbled his notes on the man's chart. 'What do you think about our patient?'

'I can't wait until we send him out of here,' she said without hesitation. 'I've never heard such a potty mouth in my life. Not only that, but he makes me uncomfortable.'

He turned to stare at her, surprised by her comment. 'Our Katie is afraid?'

'Not afraid,' she corrected. '*Uncomfortable.* There's a difference.'

He leaned back in his chair, surprised by her revelation. 'I didn't realise it bothered you to be around the prisoners.'

'It usually doesn't,' she admitted. 'This time, though…he does. Maybe it's because he attacked his guards. At any rate, I don't trust him.'

'I'd hate to get on his bad side,' J.D. agreed, recalling the man's size and muscular appearance. 'He looks like he could snap a person in two without any effort.'

He eyed Katie's slender frame and understood her reservations about being around a man who weighed three times as much as she did.

'Have you noticed how carefully he watches every move we make?' she continued. 'I'm glad they brought four officers instead of the usual two.'

'If he really bothers you, I'll get someone else—'

'I can handle it.'

Inwardly he hid a grin. Katie would never admit to a weakness. Even on hectic days, when her leg ached from an old injury, she refused to beg special consideration or lighter duty. He'd learned to watch for the tell-tale pinch around her mouth, and once it appeared he acted accordingly. Luckily, no one argued when he assigned Katie to easier tasks.

She shook her head. 'Sheldon can't do much with four deputies hovering nearby or while wearing handcuffs and belly chains.'

'By the way, I thought we replaced those old thermometers with the new ear units.'

'We did. I kept one for an emergency. Came in handy, too.'

Sheldon reappeared in the hallway, his two guards trailing behind. Once again, profanity spewed from his mouth.

'Maybe he needs his temp taken again,' J.D. commented.

Katie squared her shoulders. 'I've had just about

enough of this,' she muttered. She yanked open a drawer and removed a small tool chest.

J.D. watched her with curiosity. 'What are you going to do?'

'Watch me.' She followed Sheldon and his entourage into the exam room, with J.D. at her heels.

'Mr Sheldon,' she interrupted. 'I've heard all the foul language I care to hear.'

Thad glanced at J.D., his eyes reflecting concern over what might happen. He moved in closer, as did the other three deputies.

Katie opened the tool kit and rummaged through the screwdrivers and other assorted tools before she pulled out a tube of superglue and waved it under Sheldon's broken nose.

'Your vocabulary is offensive, not just to me but also to the other patients. I don't care what you think of me or what you say when you leave, but while you're here I expect you to clean up your act.'

Sheldon's eyes nearly bugged out of his head. Clearly he was startled by a woman half his size berating him like a child. He leaned back in an effort to put distance between himself and Katie.

'If you can't,' she informed him in a strict, schoolteacher voice, 'I'll be more than happy to use this on your mouth. Believe me, it doesn't come off easily. This is your first and final warning.'

Sheldon nodded, saying nothing.

'Fine.' Katie shoved the tube in her pocket and closed the tool chest. 'I don't want to hear a peep out of you when you're in X-Ray or when the lab girl gets here. Understand?'

Once again Sheldon nodded.

J.D. hid a grin. Katie in a temper was truly a sight

to behold. He glanced at Thad. The look of pure admiration on the officer's face, as well as on the others', was intensely satisfying.

The rest of Sheldon's stay went without incident. J.D. straightened his broken nose, stitched the cut in his forehead, determined that his ribs were intact and that the urinalysis was within normal limits.

After J.D. had cautioned Sheldon to watch for any appearance of blood in his urine, Thad and his troops herded Sheldon through the exit. Unlike his mood on his arrival, he left as meekly as the proverbial lamb.

'Ever consider working for the prison system?' J.D. asked Katie.

'No way. I can browbeat people here because they're hurting and want help. My tactics aren't nearly as effective otherwise.'

He watched her gather up her purse and coat. 'Leaving already?'

'Yup. See you later.'

For the rest of the day J.D. was too busy to dwell on his upcoming evening, but as his shift drew to a close he couldn't stop himself from watching the clock.

The moment Dr Michael Knox arrived at eight, J.D. turned over the reins without delay. He rushed home, where Daniel greeted him with enthusiasm.

'Daddy! Come see Katie's surprise!'

J.D. smiled. 'I'm coming. Did Katie finish your costume?'

Daniel grabbed one of J.D.'s hands with both of his and began tugging him through the kitchen. 'No, Daddy. You gots to close your eyes.'

J.D. let his son's grammatical error slip by. 'I am,' he said, doing as instructed.

A few steps later, Daniel released his hand as he ordered, 'You can open 'em now.'

J.D. opened his eyes, expecting to see that Katie had rearranged the furniture. To his surprise, a vision of loveliness stood before him—a vision he scarcely recognized.

He blinked, then stared again. The woman he'd expected to see—the woman he was *used* to seeing—had changed from a caterpillar to a beautiful, exotic butterfly. 'Katie?'

She giggled as she stretched out her arms. 'In the flesh.'

'What did you do to yourself?' he asked, amazed by her transformation. Her formerly straight hair was now a mass of curls. It hung to her shoulders instead of to her elbows and the colour had changed from a nondescript shade of brown to a lighter, richer golden hue resembling dark honey.

He came closer, noticing the expert application of make-up to enhance her skin tones and define her high cheek-bones. She'd painted her lips with a dusky red gloss that blended with her hair colour. Her dark eyes suddenly had become larger and more mysterious.

Her outfit was equally surprising. She'd always worn oversized T-shirts and sweatshirts while at home and shapeless scrub suits at work.

Now, however, a pair of black stretch pants revealed a willowy form and the tie around her hip-length, long-sleeved red tunic disclosed a waist he could span with both hands. The soft fabric clung to her luscious curves and the V-neckline dipped low enough to reveal a burgeoning swell.

He felt his palms itch and his mouth went dry.

Katie fluffed her hair. 'I've been thinking about a perm for a long time. My hairdresser had a cancellation and I decided it was now or never.' She lifted the ends. 'She trimmed it a little.'

A little? A foot was more accurate.

'Do you like it?' she asked.

'It's fantastic. You look like a model. I almost didn't recognise you.'

She smiled, obviously pleased with his comments and her results.

Daniel tugged on his arm. 'Isn't she pretty, Daddy?'

J.D. couldn't help but continue to stare. 'Absolutely.'

'She'll be the prettiest lady at my programme,' Daniel announced proudly.

'I think you're right,' J.D. agreed. Why had he never seen Katie before like this? He'd always thought of her as nice-looking, but he'd never really *seen* her.

He pondered the situation all throughout dinner and while Katie helped Daniel with his bath. Even by the time Daniel was safely tucked into bed, he still felt as if he'd been poleaxed.

Katie grabbed a stenographer's pad and tucked one leg under the other as she relaxed on the sofa.

'Here's the arrangement,' she began.

He paused, out of his reverie. 'What?'

She repeated herself, then went on, 'I'll help you locate suitable, eligible women, but in exchange you have to do the same for me.'

He couldn't help himself. 'You want an eligible woman, too?'

She frowned at his humour. 'No, silly. I want you to help me find a suitable, eligible male.'

'You shouldn't have any trouble finding one on your own.' Not looking like you just stepped off the cover of a magazine, he added to himself.

'No, no,' she said, shaking her head. 'It doesn't work like that. I scratch your back, you scratch mine.'

A vision of her bare back teased him.

'To paraphrase your argument to me, as a guy, you know which fellows are scumbags and which ones aren't. We'll both prepare a list of qualities we want our future spouses to have so we'll each have some guidelines to work with.'

'Aren't you rushing into this?' he asked.

She stretched out one arm along the back of the sofa and shrugged. 'You said yourself that I've given up my life, helping you. Since you're looking for a wife to take over, then I want to fill my days—and nights—with something more exciting than *Wheel of Fortune* episodes and trips to the movies with the girls.'

Because she'd turned his same arguments against him, he couldn't deny her request. He'd simply have to ignore his reluctance, especially as he didn't understand why he felt this way.

'OK. It's a deal.'

CHAPTER FOUR

KATIE swung her feet onto the floor and perched primly on the cushions. 'You go first. What qualities do you want in a woman…er…a wife?'

J.D. tried to remember the points he'd thought of throughout the day. 'Nice-looking, athletic, enjoys children in general and Daniel in particular—'

She held up one hand. Good God, she'd even had a manicure! 'Back up to "nice-looking". How nice is "nice-looking"? Are we talking passable or drop-dead gorgeous?'

'Anything that's not ugly.'

She screwed her mouth up in thought. 'OK, but just remember that beauty is in the eye of the beholder. On the same topic, do you want tall or short, skinny or with some meat on her bones, well-endowed by Mother Nature or just average in that department?'

He smiled as she chewed on her lip, ready to record his wishes. 'Tall over short, some meat on her bones, and as for the gifts of Mother Nature…' his grin broadened as her face turned a rosy hue '…if she's well proportioned, I'll be a happy man.'

His gaze landed on her own natural attributes. He would have liked to make a comparison, but he wasn't sure how the new Katie would respond so he didn't.

She jotted down a few words. 'Got it. Now, for "athletic". Are we talking about a competitive,

Olympic-medal-type person, or just someone who plays a few sports for fun?'

'Anyone who isn't averse to exercise.'

Once again she scribbled something on her pad. 'The children thing I understand. Do you want more kids?'

'If they come, fine. If they don't…' He shrugged.

'I'm curious,' she said thoughtfully. 'Are you looking for a grand passion?'

'I'm not expecting anything other than a good, solid, amenable relationship. We should have things in common, but she can have her own outside interests, too.'

She tapped her pen against the pad. 'How interesting. I hadn't figured you as the married single type.'

He frowned. 'Beg your pardon?'

'You know. You live under the same roof but go your separate ways. Once in a while you'll make an appointment and share a cappuccino. Sounds boring, but if that's what you want…' She jotted something on her notepad.

It wasn't, but he'd experienced a grand passion once before. Expecting to find the same sort of love again, that would set himself up for defeat.

'OK,' she continued. 'What about finances? Do you want her to be wealthy, average or as poor as a churchmouse? And what about her spending habits?'

'Spending habits?'

'Of course,' she said, sounding knowledgeable. 'Statistics show that the number one problem married couples face today is money. Do you want her to pinch pennies, spend lavishly or be somewhere in the middle?'

'Somewhere in the middle would be good.'

'What about working? Are you wanting her to be a stay-at-home mom?'

'It's up to her, as long as the kids don't lack for attention.'

'If she does work, are you looking for a professional—like a teacher, lawyer, doctor, and so on—or a blue-collar skilled person?'

'I didn't know Mercer had a lady lawyer in town.'

'We don't. It's a rhetorical question.'

'I'd prefer a professional.'

She paused for a moment to write again, chewing on her upper lip as she did so. Strangely enough, he hadn't noticed that particular habit before. Watching her lick her lips was oddly unsettling.

'OK,' she said brightly. 'I have a pretty good idea of what you want to get started. We'll have to fine-tune our lists as we go along because I'm sure we'll think of other things to add.'

Personally, J.D. didn't know what else could come up that hadn't been covered. Still, one never knew.

Katie flipped the page. 'Now it's my turn. Do you want me to write it down, or will you?'

'Go ahead. Your handwriting's neater.' He leaned one elbow on the chair arm to make himself comfortable, watching as Katie shifted positions.

'He should be nice-looking. He doesn't have to qualify for the cover of *Gentlemen's Quarterly* or be striking enough to turn women's heads, but he can't be so ugly that I'll worry what our children will look like.

'As for his build, I want someone about six feet two, one-eighty or -ninety. Oh, and blue eyes would be a plus.'

'Blond, too, no doubt,' he muttered, thinking of Thad.

'I'd prefer someone dark-haired, but hair colour doesn't matter. I'm not that picky,' Katie mentioned.

'Not picky?' he protested. 'Six-two, one-eighty?'

'Hey, it's my list. I can put whatever I want on it.'

'Yes, but you're limiting the possibilities.'

She tapped her pen against the pad. 'You're right. I'll scratch the blue eyes.'

Her scribbles filled the momentary silence.

'OK, then,' she said brightly, as if enjoying herself. 'I don't mind if he's athletic or is an avid fan, but I refuse to be a football or golf or baseball widow. I enjoy watching televised events and attending them on occasion, but I won't let my life revolve around whatever sport is in season.'

'Fair enough.'

'As for kids, I don't mind if he enters into our marriage with children, but I want at least two of my own. I want him to be willing to teach them how to ride a bike, play baseball or participate in whatever activity they're interested in. He has to take an active role in their lives, not just come home at night and be a couch potato.'

'Think you'll find someone like that?'

'You're the one who's doing the looking,' she reminded him. 'As for his job, it doesn't matter.' She nibbled on the end of her pen. 'I take that back. No medical people. Manual labourers are good— they have great pecs.'

He wouldn't have been more surprised if she'd asked for a ballet dancer. 'No medical people? Why not?'

'Because he'll want to talk shop all the time. When I'm at home I want to leave my job at the hospital.' She paused. 'Come to think of it, you probably don't know many men who don't have ties to health care, do you?'

'Not many,' he admitted. He knew his neighbours, his barber, the guys at the garage who worked on his van from time to time. Not a large pool to draw from.

'A professional of some sort would be nice,' she said. 'Maybe even someone in law enforcement. There's something about a man in a uniform...'

'I've heard women go for that,' he said, remembering Thad and feeling as if he didn't measure up in some indefinable way.

'Unlike you, I want a grand passion and romance. I want the flowers, the candy, the whole shebang. Just like in the movies.'

'Poetry, too, I suppose.' Where in the world would he find someone who met *this* standard?

'It would be nice, but it's not mandatory.'

She tore off her page and handed it to him. 'There you go. Happy hunting.'

'I could say the same to you. By the way, have you thought about how you're going to meet these guys? I mean, I can call up a woman and ask her out, but what about you?'

She appeared affronted. 'Who says I can't do the same?'

He blinked. The lamb had changed into a lioness. 'No one. I just thought—'

'Actually,' she interrupted smoothly, 'I thought you could just give me the names and I'll take it from there. If he's someone I don't know, then you can introduce me.'

She'd obviously formed her game plan. 'I suppose that would work.'

'Of course it will.' Katie glanced at the clock resting on top of the entertainment centre. 'Gosh, it's late. I'd better go.'

'It's only ten.'

'Yes, but some of us need our beauty rest. Besides, I want to make a few phone calls first thing in the morning. The sooner we start working on our little project, the better. Wouldn't you agree?'

Now he understood what a whirlwind was like. Somehow he'd lost control of the situation.

Later, as he studied her neat handwriting and pondered her requirements for a husband, he had one question.

What had he got himself into?

J.D. reported to work first thing Monday morning expecting the usual organised chaos. In the past he'd have listened to Dr Knox's summary of the past twelve hours, but today the conversation revolved around Katie.

'Have you seen her?' Michael asked him, his eyes wide with undisguised interest. 'She looks like a million dollars.'

Possessiveness rose up in J.D. 'Yeah, she does, and yes, I saw her this weekend.'

'If I were single, I'd request a change of shifts or ask her to transfer to mine.' Michael winked.

'Yeah, well, you're not, Dr Daddy-to-be,' J.D. said dryly.

Michael shrugged good-naturedly. 'Mark my words, once the word gets out you'll have every young buck in the hospital dropping by for one reason or another.'

J.D. didn't doubt it. The diamond in the rough had been cut and polished and now every prospective buyer would come around to inspect the merchandise.

What they *didn't* know, he thought with satisfaction, was that they'd have to go through him. This gem wouldn't go to just anyone and most especially not to someone who was only interested in her appearance. He would find someone worthy of her and none of the single men he knew at the moment seemed good enough for Katie Alexander.

For the rest of the morning Michael's prediction came true. The steady stream of visitors asking for Katie didn't stop even while she was at lunch. Feeling like her social secretary, J.D.'s mood darkened.

He had just sent a respiratory therapist on his way moments before Katie returned. Her dazzling smile did nothing to restore his good humour. Had she always been so bubbly or smelled like a field of fresh flowers?

He still couldn't believe this vision was the same woman he'd known for the past four years. It seemed impossible for a person to change so drastically in such a short time, but she had. To think she'd been under his nose, in plain sight, and he hadn't noticed.

He took some consolation in that he wasn't the only one who'd overlooked her desirability.

'About time,' he groused. 'Another admirer stopped by to see you.'

'Really?' she asked. 'Who was it?'

'Blackwell in RT. Before him, it was Smith from Central Supply and Andrews in Maintenance.'

'Did they say what they wanted?'

He gave her his exasperated look. 'No, but I have a good idea and it doesn't concern hospital business.'

She smiled. 'I know it's bothersome, but I'm glad they're dropping into ER.'

'Like flies,' he said gloomily.

Katie giggled. 'It's not that bad. Look at the bright side. You'll be able to screen them for me, remember?'

Not giving him time to reply, she placed a small, square, pink sticky-note in front of him. 'Speaking of screening, you don't know what I went through to get this for you.'

He picked up the paper. 'What is it?'

'Your first candidate's phone number. I also happen to know she's not busy this evening.'

He eyed the seven digits recorded in Katie's flowing hand. 'Who's the lady?' he asked, curious about the woman Katie had deemed acceptable.

'Cecilia Garnett. You know her. She's one of the pharmacists.'

He recognised the name. 'The Dolly Parton look-alike?'

She smiled, as if knowing that Cecilia's hair wasn't the part of her anatomy known to draw men's attention. 'That's her.'

'And she's free tonight?'

Katie nodded. 'When I was coming back from lunch I overheard her talking to her co-worker. I stopped to visit, which is why I'm late, but I found out something helpful,' she added triumphantly. 'She loves to go to the movies so you won't have to think of an outing.'

'Movies are good,' he said. 'What's playing?'

'Jim Carrey's latest, along with a Harrison Ford adventure and one of those horror flicks. Take your pick.'

He didn't have any problem making a decision; Harrison Ford was his favourite actor. 'We'll have to go to the late show,' he said, thinking aloud. 'I'll also need to find someone to watch Daniel…'

'I'm not finished with his costume so I'll sit with him until you get home,' she offered.

'Then it's settled. I'll call her right now.'

J.D. reached for the phone, but she stayed his hand. 'I wouldn't ask her out now. Not unless you want the entire hospital to know.'

'What do you suggest? Send a note through the hospital information system?' He'd never realised how soft Katie's skin felt.

Katie rolled her eyes. 'No. She leaves work in an hour. Call her then. Otherwise she'll be so excited she'll announce to everyone she sees that you've asked her for a date.'

'Won't they hear anyway?' He'd already resigned himself to the news spreading through the hospital faster than chickenpox through a roomful of children. In fact, he was counting on it. The rumours would serve to show his intent on planting roots in the community.

'Yes, but why advertise before the fact?'

He pulled his hand back, the imprint of her fingers feeling indelibly etched on his wrist. The reasons for his reaction puzzled him.

Had the fact that he was seeing Katie in a new light making everything about her seem fresh and new? It was something he'd have to think about.

'OK. I'll call her in an hour.'

'Good.' Katie seemed satisfied. 'Don't forget.'

'I won't.' He studied her for a long moment. 'You don't know how much I appreciate this.'

Her smile was broad. 'My pleasure. Any luck on finding a date for me?'

'I'm still checking out a few people.'

'OK.' She seemed satisfied by his response so he didn't mention how her detailed list of qualifications had narrowed the choices.

The radio squawked and Katie immediately reached for the handset and identified herself.

'We have a sixteen-year-old girl with possible acute alcohol poisoning,' the disembodied male voice reported. 'BP is 160 over 80, pulse is 95. ETA is two minutes.'

'Ten four,' Katie responded crisply before she signed off the air.

J.D. had seen a few of Mercer's teenagers come in on Friday nights drunker than the proverbial skunks, but rarely during the week and never during school time.

'Who's handling the psychiatry consults?' he asked.

Katie glanced at a posted schedule. 'Dr Davidson. Dr Patterson is out of town. Do you want me to notify him?'

'Not yet,' J.D. decided.

But when the ambulance arrived and two EMTs and a city police officer carted in a young girl reeking of alcohol, J.D. knew he had no choice.

'She says her name is Bobbie Rumsey,' Doug Schroeder, a technician in his late twenties, reported. 'She was walking through the park and collapsed. A passerby saw her and called 911.'

'We'll need to notify her parents,' J.D. said.

The police officer, a tall, athletic-appearing redhead with GILES engraved on his name tag, interrupted. 'Her mother is on her way. The father is a truck driver and is out of town.'

Satisfied by their efforts, J.D. addressed Bobbie. 'What were you drinking?'

'Don't know.' Her speech was slurred, her face flushed. She tried to brush the hair away from her face, but her arm fell onto the gurney as if she didn't have the strength. She certainly didn't have the co-ordination.

'Did you take any pills?'

Bobbie didn't respond, and J.D. leaned closer to her ears before repeating himself in a louder voice.

She winced. 'Don't have to yell,' she mumbled. 'Heard you the first time. Can't remember. Think so.'

'How many? What kind?'

Bobbie waved her hand in careless abandon. 'Headache stuff.'

J.D. spoke to Katie. 'Let's get a urine drug screen, blood alcohol, acetaminophen and salicylate levels, along with the usual CBC and electrolytes.' He turned to the EMTs, whom he knew on a first-name basis. 'Any idea on where she got the alcohol?'

Doug and his partner, Myron, both shook their heads. 'She didn't have anything with her when we arrived.'

'I'll need to question her,' Officer Giles said. 'It's illegal for a minor to purchase liquor and if someone bought it for her, he or she can be prosecuted as well.'

The lab technician appeared on the scene with her tray of supplies. At the sight of the woman's needle and the colourful array of tubes, waiting to be filled, Bobbie's attitude changed to fear.

'Leave me alone. Don't take my blood.' Bobbie turned her head toward J.D. 'She'll hurt me,' she whined. 'Don't hurt me.'

'We won't,' J.D. said firmly. 'The pain will only last a few moments and won't be any worse than a mosquito bite. Just hold still.'

Bobbie sniffled. 'She'll hurt me.'

J.D. took Bobbie's hand in his. 'No, she won't.' He gave the technician a nod to proceed. 'It will be over before you know it.'

He talked to Bobbie throughout the entire procedure, alternating his running commentary on how much longer the procedure would be with praise for how well she was doing. As soon as the tech finished, J.D. patted Bobbie's shoulder.

'That wasn't so bad, was it?'

Tears spilled down Bobbie's cheeks. J.D. took the tissue Katie held out and handed it to the girl.

'Just rest. Your mother will be here soon.'

At this news, Bobbie's tears turned into a veritable shower. 'She's not my mother!' she blubbered. 'Debbie won't come. I'm in the way. She wants to get rid of me.'

J.D. exchanged a glance with Katie before he addressed the others. 'Why don't you leave us alone with her for a few minutes?'

From the look on Doug's and Myron's faces, they were more than happy to oblige, although J.D. didn't miss the sidelong glances they bestowed on Katie before they exited.

'Is that what this is all about?' J.D. asked her. 'You're not getting along with your stepmother?'

A tearful Bobbie poured her story out in halting sentences. She'd just been cut from the basketball team, her boyfriend had broken up with her and she was flunking algebra. Her mother had died a year ago, and her dad—whose job took him on the road most of the time—had remarried several months later. His new wife seemed uninterested in her stepdaughter and Bobbie now apparently felt adrift.

Desperate, she'd found a bottle of whiskey in a cupboard and had proceeded to drink herself into a stupor.

Knowing Katie had experienced the loss of her mother at about the same age, J.D. didn't argue when she signalled for him to leave. Armed with this knowledge, he hoped to visit with the new Mrs Rumsey as soon as she arrived.

The officer stopped him in the hallway. 'How long do you think it will be until I can talk to her?'

'Not long. Bobbie admitted that she found a bottle of her dad's whiskey. It's the classic story. Her problems seemed insurmountable and she wanted to escape.'

Giles nodded, as if he agreed. 'Unfortunately, it happens so often these days. At least she didn't pull a trigger.'

J.D. concurred. Having seen enough attempted suicides in his ER stints to last a lifetime, he hoped Bobbie hadn't mixed other substances with the alcohol she'd already imbibed.

Giles turned to leave, then stopped. 'The nurse, Katie? I haven't seen her around here before. Is she new?'

J.D. bit back a sigh. The changes in Katie made her appear like a totally new person, but he didn't like the idea of another man joining her rapidly swelling ranks of admirers. 'She's worked here for years.'

'I've only been in town a few months myself,' Giles said. 'Is she seeing anybody?'

J.D. studied the man through critical eyes. The policeman looked like a poster Marine and fitted her requirements of six feet two and one-eighty. While J.D. stayed as active and physically fit as possible, his efforts seemed insignificant in comparison. Katie would, no doubt, spend her hours at the health club, watching Giles maintain those rock-hard muscles.

He intended to dissuade him, but before he could do so the officer's face lit up.

J.D. turned to watch Katie approach. He took heart from her lack of response to the man's obvious adoration.

'She's calm now,' she said, 'but I hope you're going to refer her to the mental health centre for counselling.'

Her fierce tone reminded him of a hen looking after her chicks.

'I'm on my way to do that right now.'

A brunette in her late thirties rushed up to them.

'I was told that Bobbie Rumsey is here. I'm her stepmother, Debra.'

'I'm Dr Berkley. You can see her in a few minutes, but first we need to discuss her condition.'

J.D. pulled her aside to a somewhat private spot in the hallway, while Katie—and Officer Giles—headed for the nurses' desk. He forced the picture of the two together out of his mind in order to focus on the case at hand.

Debra's face had paled. 'Is she OK? She said she didn't feel well this morning so I called the school and told them she was sick. What happened? Did she call 911?'

J.D. explained the situation, finishing with the observation 'She thinks you don't care about her.'

Debra rubbed her forehead as she stared at the floor. 'I do,' she said hoarsely. 'Her mother was a friend of mine and I thought…well, it doesn't matter what I thought. I've heard stories of kids resenting their step-parents so I didn't want to push her.'

'Apparently she took your actions as a sign that you didn't care,' J.D. commented.

Debra's shoulders slumped. 'I suppose. I'm not good at this mothering stuff. I've never been married before or been around children, much less teenagers, for any length of time.'

She gave a wan smile. 'Visiting with other people's kids isn't the same.'

He remembered his own turmoil when he'd first faced the responsibility of Daniel's care. His personal experience with youngsters had been limited to the family gatherings of his friends where he'd acted as a benevolent uncle.

'No, it's not,' he agreed. 'But don't be so hard on

yourself. What's important is how you're going to deal with the situation from now on. Bobbie—maybe your whole family—would benefit from seeing a counsellor or therapist.'

A short distance away, he saw Katie wave a sheet of paper in the air. To J.D.'s relief, Giles was noticeably absent. In his opinion, Officer Giles should be spending his time on the streets of Mercer ferreting out criminals rather than romancing J.D.'s nurse.

'If you'd like to see her, you can,' he told Debra, certain that Bobbie's lab results were waiting for his review. 'She's in Room Three.'

A minute later, he took the reports from Katie, once again distinguishing her scent from the usual hospital odour. 'New perfume, too?' he asked, trying to understand why he was noticing something he hadn't before.

'Nope. Same old stuff. I see the drug screens were negative, except for the alcohol.'

He clipped the pages inside Bobbie's medical record. 'Yeah. The levels aren't toxic, so I'll send her home.'

'After you put the fear of God into her, I hope.'

J.D. grinned. 'Of course. A lecture is included in our emergency room fee.'

As he entered their cubicle he was pleased to find Debra and Bobbie holding hands. With luck, and the guidance of a professional, he hoped this episode would mark a turning point in their relationship.

'Alcohol was the only drug the lab found,' he told Debra.

'Thank God,' she said in a heartfelt manner.

'I'll forego my standard drug lecture as it

wouldn't make an impression right now,' he said, looking at his dozing patient.

Mrs Rumsey's gaze followed his as she nodded.

'I'm sure the counsellor will cover all the points I would, anyway.'

'I'm making an appointment as soon as we get home,' she promised. 'And I intend to remind her that if she wants to play sports, she can't do something stupid like this again.'

J.D. grinned. It appeared that Debra's days of permissive motherhood were over. And, thinking of appointments, he had one of his own to make.

After releasing Bobbie, he dropped her records at the desk.

'Well?' Katie demanded.

'I think they're going to be fine,' he reported. 'Mrs Rumsey will call the centre as soon as they get home.'

'Good.' Apparently noticing that he wasn't stopping to make chit-chat, she asked, 'Where are you going?'

'To use a *private* phone.'

'Oh, yeah.'

A few minutes later he was speaking to Cecilia and making arrangements to pick her up in time for the early show. Somewhat ill-at-ease about stepping into the dating arena after being out of circulation for so long, he took her cheerful voice to be a good omen for a pleasant evening.

'It was the most uncomfortable evening I've ever had,' J.D. told Katie as he plopped onto his recliner around ten o'clock the same night.

Seated in front of the sewing machine, Katie

turned around in her straight-backed chair to stare at him with wide eyes. 'You are home earlier than I'd expected. What went wrong?'

'What went right?' he said glumly. 'From the moment I got there she talked so much I couldn't get a word in edgewise.'

'She must have been nervous about making a good impression. You have a tendency to make people tense, you know.'

He shot her a look of disgust. 'I don't believe it.'

'Sure, you do. Look at Ashley. She gets flustered whenever you're around.'

'I thought she was normally scatterbrained.'

'Nope. She's afraid of making a mistake under your eagle eye. She tries too hard to be perfect and her efforts backfire.'

He narrowed his eyes. 'So, if I can drive people into becoming blithering idiots, why don't you quiver and quake in my presence?'

Her giggle made him smile. 'You remind me of my brother, Gideon. I learned early on that his bark was worse than his bite. You're the same way. Don't worry, though. I won't tell anyone.'

She continued. 'Back to Cecilia. How could she talk all the time? You went to the movies, didn't you?'

J.D. stretched out his legs and crossed his ankles. 'Yeah, but she kept telling me what was going to happen next. If she was right she bragged about it, and if she was wrong she ridiculed the producers. I've never heard anyone so critical in my life.'

'Maybe it was just a bad film. Which one did you see?'

'The horror picture.'

A look of stunned surprise crossed her face. 'Horror? You? Dr I've-seen-all-the-blood-and-guts-I-want-to-see Berkley?'

'Yeah, me,' he said, recognising her quote of his famous excuse for avoiding those sorts of motion pictures. 'Being the nice guy that I am, I gave in. Unfortunately, her talking wasn't the worst part.'

'Oh?'

He shook his head. 'If we hadn't had an armrest separating our seats, I'm sure she would have been in my lap.' Apparently Cecilia thought the feel of her ample breasts against his forearm was her idea of letting him know she wanted her evening to include more than a movie and a drink.

He should have enjoyed it—and probably would have if the vision of Katie and Daniel sending him off with a wave and the admonition to have a good time hadn't interfered.

Somehow he knew they hadn't meant for him to accept Cecilia's invitation to try out her feather bed.

'What a shame,' Katie said, not sounding particularly disappointed to J.D.'s ears. 'I thought you two would do well together.'

'You were wrong.'

'Back to the drawing board.'

'I'd say so.'

'I'll add ''shy and retiring'' to your list of qualifications,' she said.

'Fine.' He motioned to the bundle of fabric on the little table he'd purchased to hold her machine. 'How's the costume coming?'

'Almost finished,' she said, holding it up for his view. 'Daniel's so excited about Hallowe'en that he could hardly settle down and go to sleep.'

'It's still two weeks away!'

She smiled. 'Yeah. Anticipation is half the fun. If it's OK with you, Daniel and I will trick-or-treat to the hospital. Then you can walk him back and catch the houses we missed on your way home.'

He frowned, puzzled by her arrangement. 'You don't want to go with us?'

'It's not that I don't want to. I have to be home by nine.' She paused to nibble on her lip. 'I have a date.'

CHAPTER FIVE

J.D. FROZE. 'A date? I thought I was supposed to screen the guys first.'

Katie blushed a becoming shade of pink, then lowered her head to study the seam she was pinning together. 'Yeah, well, it just came up.'

'Who is he?'

'Hank Giles.'

The name immediately rang a bell. 'The policeman?'

She nodded. 'He seems like a nice guy, don't you think?'

'I guess. It's hard to say after only talking to him in a professional context for a few minutes.'

'He's invited me to a Hallowe'en party. One of his fellow officers is hosting it.'

'A costume party?'

'Yeah. He suggested we go as a football player and cheerleader, but I'm not too sure...' Her voice died.

Instinctively, J.D. understood she was referring to her leg. While the scars left from an accident during her teenage years didn't bother him in the slightest, other people were ill at ease around those with imperfections.

'So be something else,' he said bluntly. 'Like Red Riding Hood and the Big Bad Wolf.'

She chuckled. 'Somehow I get the feeling you don't like Hank.'

'It doesn't have anything to do with like or dislike,' he insisted. 'You deserve better.'

'Better than a respected member of the police force? A man dedicated to restoring law and order?' Her eyes narrowed slightly. 'Or is it because *you* didn't stamp him with your seal of approval?'

'OK, I'll admit it,' he said, wondering why he was being so critical of the man. 'If you want me to screen your dates, you have to give me time.'

'How much time do you need? Need I remind you how I've followed through on my part of the agreement and you haven't? In case this detail has escaped you, we both have the same number of hours in our day.'

'Yes, but Cecilia didn't work out.'

'Hey, that's not my fault,' she protested. 'I said I'd find women who matched your criteria. Period. I can't help it if there's no chemistry. I'm doing my best and I expect you to do the same.'

'For your information, I've made some enquiries. Milt Hayes is interested in finding a date for the hospital's fall picnic, day after tomorrow. If you'd like, I'll let him know you're available.'

She thought a moment, as if considering his suggestion. 'OK.' Rising, she continued before he could answer. 'Now that I think about it, you should give Marilyn Stafford a call.'

'The new medical librarian?' he asked, watching her flip through the telephone directory.

Katie jotted something on the scratch pad next to the telephone, then handed him the note. 'Yes. She's so nice. Quiet, too. Marilyn will be perfect.'

He stared at the phone number and address. 'You're sure she won't be another Cecilia?'

'Definitely. They're total opposites. Like night and day.'

The morning after his date with Marilyn, J.D. physically pulled Katie into the first vacant exam cubicle. 'Your comment about Cecilia and Marilyn being like day and night was right on target.'

A satisfied smile appeared on her face. 'What did I tell you?'

He gave her an exasperated look. 'Do you suppose you could recommend someone more like "noon"?'

Her perfectly shaped eyebrows dipped together in puzzlement. 'What do you mean?'

'Cecilia talked non-stop. Trying to have a conversation with Marilyn, it was like pulling teeth. Most of the time I was talking to myself.'

'I told you she was quiet.'

'Aren't there any women out there who don't go to extremes?'

She crossed her arms over her cheery pink scrub suit. 'Thanks a lot, buster. And which group do I fit in?'

'I didn't mean you,' he said, backpedalling.

'Really?' Katie didn't seem convinced. 'Then why don't I ask if there are any men out there who aren't anxious to jump in the sack just because they paid for your dinner?'

'Ah,' he said, understanding why Katie was as out of sorts as he was. 'Milt didn't work out?'

'You should have warned me about his octopusal tendencies.'

'Octopusal? Is that a word?'

'If it isn't, it should be,' she declared. 'It describes

him perfectly. After we left the picnic, he drove me home. By the time I got there I felt like I'd been in a wrestling match.'

He was aghast. 'I didn't have any idea he would try anything.' To be honest, he was indignant on Katie's behalf. He revised his opinion of Milt by lowering it several notches.

She sighed. 'I know. I apologise for taking my frustrations out on you. Better luck next time, right?'

'Right.'

Ashley poked her head into the room. 'I hate to interrupt, but we need you. An ambulance is on its way with a trauma.'

'How bad?' J.D. asked.

'A woodcutting accident,' Ashley reported. 'He gashed his lower leg right above the ankle.'

J.D. winced, recalling one situation during his training when a man had managed to saw off several toes instead of tree branches. To this day he couldn't understand how it had happened but he wasn't interested in re-enacting the scene.

'Put him in Trauma One,' he ordered.

'Can't,' she replied. 'We have a kid in there from the high school. We're waiting for the orthopaedic guy to get here for an evaluation.'

'What about Trauma Two?' he asked.

'Dr Roswell is using it for one of his patients. A possible ectopic pregnancy.'

Once again J.D. wished for the ER to be enlarged and more rooms outfitted for trauma cases.

'Room Three is open,' Ashley volunteered brightly.

The four exam rooms were close quarters even if only the patient, one family member and a staff member were present. It would be especially cosy to have two nurses assisting.

'Put Paul Bunyan in there,' he said reluctantly. 'Meanwhile, let's hope we won't get any more traumas until the other rooms clear out again.'

By the time Katie and Ashley had laid out the more basic supplies and the three of them had slipped on their yellow protective gowns, face shields and gloves, the ectopic pregnancy case had been admitted for emergency surgery.

Moments before the ambulance arrived with their patient, J.D. instructed Katie to reroute him to the now-vacant trauma room.

Roy Barker, a man in his late twenties, lay strapped to the gurney with his pant leg slit open to above his knee. In spite of the bandages and elevation of his left leg, the pressure pad above his ankle was soaked with blood. His clothing hadn't gone unscathed—his dust-covered jeans and blue plaid flannel shirt were liberally spattered with dark red, wet-looking blotches.

As they carted Roy into the trauma room, the two paramedics J.D. knew well—Doug and Myron—recited the listing of vital signs. A worried young woman followed at a discreet distance.

'What happened?' J.D. asked as he studied the scope of the wound before he undid the pressure bandages.

A faint sheen of perspiration dotted Roy's upper lip. 'I was almost finished when my chain saw ran out of gas. I had a few pieces I wanted to break into kindling so I got out the axe. It slipped and here I am.'

'Ouch.' J.D. turned to Ashley. 'I want a CBC and a basic chem. panel.'

While she left the bedside to make the arrangements, J.D. faced his patient and began making small talk to help his patient relax. 'Were you at home?'

Roy rubbed his eyes with one hand as he spoke. 'Yeah. My wife and I live right outside of town. We have a few acres.'

The woman stepped forward to stand near Roy's head. Taking one hand, she threaded her fingers through his. 'Our property has a shelter belt and we've been trying to clean out the dead trees.'

'You were with him?'

'Yes.' She stroked Roy's forehead, rearranging a fallen lock of hair. 'Good thing, too. His shoe was filled with blood and he couldn't walk by himself. I couldn't get him into the car so I called 911.'

She paused. 'I knew we should have hired a professional tree service to handle everything. It would have been cheaper in the long run and less wearing on my nerves.'

J.D. exchanged a knowing glance with Katie. 'You're not the first one who's come to that conclusion,' he said. 'And, unfortunately, you won't be the last.'

He lifted one corner of the bandages and blood immediately welled up in the four-inch long-cut which went through muscle.

'This is going to be messy,' he told his patient as he replaced the pad. 'I'm afraid your jeans won't be salvageable.'

'My clothes are the least of my worries,' Roy said weakly.

J.D. fell silent as he began checking for any nerve or vascular damage. The steady pulse and slightly pink toes suggested adequate circulation.

He touched the arch of Roy's foot. 'Can you feel this?'

'Yes, sir.'

J.D. reached for the syringes Katie had prepared and was holding out for his use. 'We'll give you something for the pain and a local anaesthetic before we get started.'

'How bad is it?' Mrs Barker asked.

'I don't think we'll need an emergency vascular surgeon consult.'

The worry on her face seemed to lessen.

Immediately after J.D. had injected the syringes' contents, the lab tech arrived to collect her samples. By the time the drugs began to take effect, the technician was on her way out the door.

J.D. lifted the blood-soaked bandage away from the laceration. He spoke to Roy and his wife as he worked quickly and with Katie's assistance to halt the dark red flow.

'Just like I thought. It doesn't appear as if you nicked the artery,' he commented casually, although he felt sympathy pains for the man.

Without waiting for their response, he continued as he irrigated the wound with saline. 'I'm washing out the cut to make sure there aren't any wood chips hanging around inside to cause an infection.'

After cleansing the torn tissue with an antiseptic solution, he began suturing the layers together. 'Good thing you were wearing boots,' he said as he guided the needle through muscle and skin. 'Otherwise, you'd have done a lot more damage.'

By the time the lab telephoned with the results, J.D. had finished his task. While the CBC showed a lower haemoglobin than expected in a healthy male, it hadn't dropped to a level requiring a transfusion.

He scribbled his notes and observations on Roy's chart, before giving the couple last-minute instructions and a prescription for pain medication.

Upon entering the hallway, he saw Doug and Myron talking to Katie and overheard part of their conversation.

'It's great to have you on board,' the paramedic said enthusiastically, his face wreathed in smiles. 'You won't regret it.' With that, he and his partner guided the gurney through the doors toward the ambulance.

J.D. moved in closer. 'What's he talking about?'

She strode into the supply closet and began opening cabinets and removing extra gowns. 'You remember how the ambulance service lost three of their EMTs in the last month?'

He followed her and stood on the threshold. 'Yeah. So?'

'I'm going to help them out.'

He narrowed his eyes in suspicion. 'What do you mean by "help them out"?'

'I'm going to work with them on my days off until the department hires permanent replacements.'

He was stunned. 'You're joking.'

'No, I'm not.'

'Why?'

'Why not?' she countered.

'I can think of several reasons.'

She faced him and folded her arms across her chest. 'Oh, really?'

'You're a nurse.'

'I was an emergency medical technician first.'

He thought fast and worded his objections carefully. 'You haven't ridden an ambulance for as long as I've known you. Procedures have changed.'

She shrugged, seemingly unconcerned. 'I've kept my certification current. Just because I have my nursing degree, it doesn't mean I've forgotten what's expected of an EMT. If anything, I'll be better than ever.'

'Think of the physical demands. It won't be easy on you.'

'You mean because I have a bum knee?'

'Well…' He grimaced, certain he was about to put his proverbial foot in his mouth. 'Yes.'

'My leg is fine.' She enunciated each word.

'I didn't mean to offend you, but how are you going to carry three-hundred-pound fellows?'

'You're confusing me with the firemen. I don't bring people out of burning buildings on my back.'

He dismissed her with a wave. 'All right, then. *Lift.* How are you going to lift patients who are bigger than you are?'

'The same way I do here,' she said. 'Very carefully. Besides, we both know that there are always other people around to help. I can handle whatever is necessary.'

'Won't that put an extra burden on your partner? He's not going to want to do all the grunt work.'

She visibly bristled. 'Your confidence in my abilities is astounding. If they didn't think I could do the job, they wouldn't have hired me.'

Obviously warming to her subject, she poked a finger in his chest. 'For your information, the guys came to *me*, asking for my help. Not the other way around.'

'I stand corrected, but—'

'There are no buts, J.D. I really don't know why you're making such a fuss. I'm helping out for one or two days a week to cover for their well-deserved days off. It's only for a month or two, not indefinitely.'

He changed tactics. 'But Daniel and I won't have a chance to see you. He's counting on you going trick-or-treating with him and attending his pre-school programme.'

'I'll be around to do those things.' She turned away to check the contents of the small refrigerator. 'As for not seeing me, you're looking for a wife, remember? Have you considered how Daniel will adjust to another woman in your life if I'm always around? It's not good to send him mixed signals.'

Her comment hung in the air like a cloud of thick, heavy smoke. The woman he married would take over the role Katie had assumed and Katie's presence in their lives would gradually diminish.

The thought wasn't a happy one.

With blinding insight, J.D. realised what his quest for a wife would cost both him and Daniel.

He didn't like the price tag.

What if he married Katie? The idea packed as powerful a punch as the one before. It echoed in his mind until he thought he might have spoken it aloud. But Katie's expression didn't change, so he obviously hadn't.

His heart raced as another notion came to him.

Was this why he'd found her transformation into a beautiful, desirable woman so startling? Had he grown so used to her that it had taken a drastic change to see her with new eyes?

Instinctively, he knew he was right.

By her own admission, Katie was looking for a husband. Would she consider him as husband material?

He'd never been afraid to discuss any subject with her, yet this question seemed too shocking to pose out of the blue. Impulsively changing the foundation of their relationship, that could spell disaster to their friendship.

Logically, however, his plan made perfect sense. They got along well together, knew each other's idiosyncrasies and habits, and shared interests. Why hadn't he thought of this before now?

Before he could pat himself on the back for his idea, he recalled the list of qualities she wanted in her dream husband. She'd asked for a man who was totally different from J.D. in looks, temperament and profession. J.D. didn't have a chance.

The idea was totally disconcerting.

Katie squared her shoulders. 'You can scowl all you like, but I'm not changing my mind. Helping the ambulance service is what I want to do.'

Not aware he'd been frowning, he quickly changed his expression and his tactics. 'I'm just trying to figure out when you'll have time to husband-hunt.'

'I'll still have at least five evenings free. Unless you have a ton of prospects waiting in the wings, I can't see where I'll have a problem,' she said wryly.

Sensing it was time to retreat and fine-tune his

strategy, he did. 'All right. But promise that if the job gets to be too much for you, you'll quit, regardless of whether they've hired replacements or not.'

Her smile grew bright. 'I promise.'

He left her to her cupboards, irritatingly aware of the hunks who worked in the city's EMS programme. The teasing remarks he'd overheard, the recent gazes of admiration, the flattering little nicknames—every incident took on serious connotations. He had to do something, and soon.

Perhaps he could stack the deck in his favour. A few more dates like Milt—not *exactly* like Milt, he amended, disliking the notion of any other man's hands roaming on *his* Katie—and she would see that J.D. was the perfect candidate for marriage.

He thought of the men he'd dismissed before as being unsuitable. While they possessed some of her qualifying traits, they also had what he considered to be a fatal flaw. Now that he considered the matter, matching her with these fellows would only help his cause. In the process, she was sure to modify her list of requirements.

However, if this plan didn't work, he held one advantage over his competitors. He had Daniel.

'I'm surprised we don't have a single patient,' Lee Tucker, an ER nurse, commented on Hallowe'en night.

J.D. grinned. 'I think a kid would have to be half-dead before they'd admit to being sick this evening. Can't miss out on all the fun.'

He glanced at the clock. A quarter to eight. Katie and Daniel should be arriving soon. With any luck, his replacement, Michael, would get here first.

The pendulum doors swung open and he watched with bated breath, hoping he could get away before a patient ruined his plans. Daniel would never forgive him if Katie had to leave for her date and he had to spend his evening waiting at the hospital because J.D. didn't have a sitter.

A miniature but fierce-looking Captain Hook, holding hands with a beautiful Peter Pan, brought a smile to his face. He skirted the desk to stand in front of the pair, noticing Peter Pan's extremely short tunic. His gaze travelled along the miles of long legs clad in green opaque tights that clung like a second skin but hid any and all blemishes.

His breath left him for a few seconds, but he quickly recovered. 'Who do we have here?' he asked in mock surprise. 'Another patient?'

Captain Hook giggled, then stared up at Peter Pan. 'Daddy doesn't know who I am,' he said in a loud whisper.

'Of course not. Our disguises are too good,' she said.

'Oh, my goodness, Doctor,' Lee said, joining in the spirit of things. 'He's had an accident. Well, Captain Hook, you came to the right place. Dr Berkley will fix your arm right up.'

Hook giggled once again. 'Don't want to be fixed.'

J.D. crouched down to Captain Hook's level. 'You don't?'

Hook shook his head so hard his eyepatch slipped down one paint-smeared cheek. He pushed it back in place. 'No. We're here 'cause it's Hallowe'en. Trick or treat?' he chanted in a sing-song voice.

'Well, then. Do we have some treats to give out?' J.D. asked Lee.

Lee looked around the desk before he opened a drawer and pulled out a bag of lollipops. Leaning over the counter to hand several to Daniel, he asked, 'Will this do?'

Captain Hook bobbed his head and once again his eyepatch slipped. Before he could push it into place, J.D. peered into his face. 'Daniel, is that you?'

Daniel giggled. 'Yes, Daddy. It's me.' He pointed to Peter Pan. 'And that's Katie.'

Lee gave a wolf whistle. 'Golly, Miss Molly. Katie, you *do* have legs.'

Katie smoothed the fabric of her costume over her thighs. 'Of course I do. Same as everyone else.'

'Yeah, but we never get to see yours.'

'Now you know how I feel,' she teased.

'I'll wear shorts the next time you're on duty. Mine don't look as good, though,' Lee mourned.

She flung up her hands. 'What can I say? Eat your heart out.'

Michael Knox strode through the doors. 'What's this about a heart?'

'We're discussing Katie's legs,' Lee informed him.

Michael stopped in his tracks as he, too, inspected her form. 'Whoa, there. Good thing you don't come to work like that. We'd be inundated with every male in the county.'

Katie's face turned pink.

'I'll bet J.D. will agree with me,' he continued.

Because J.D. didn't like the idea of Lee and Michael—or *any* man other than himself—ogling Katie's legs, he quickly answered, 'Yeah, well, it's getting late and I'll bet Captain Hook has a lot more houses to visit.'

Daniel nodded. 'My bucket is only half-full. It has to be full before we can stop.'

'Now, Daniel, we mustn't be greedy,' Katie gently chided.

'I just want enough to share with my friends at pre-school,' Daniel defended himself, staring up at her. ''Sides, I'm bigger than last year so I can eat more.'

J.D. peered into the pumpkin bucket. 'From the looks of things, you have plenty, now.' At Daniel's groan, he added, 'I suppose a few more pieces won't hurt. Shall we go?'

He quickly ushered them out of the hospital, nodding politely to the staff members who smiled and waved at them.

The evening couldn't have been more beautiful if they'd special-ordered it. The cool night air carried only a breath of a breeze. The full, yellow-orange moon hung low in the sky. Streetlamps lit the corners of every tree-lined block and beams from flashlights crisscrossed yards as children darted from one house to the next.

Daniel joined the ranks of a princess, a dinosaur, a beggar and a mummy going towards a welcoming home. Their small feet shuffled through the dry leaves as they cut across the grass in their rush to be the first to ring the doorbell.

J.D. stayed near the kerb with Katie, holding the flashlight and watching the entourage proclaim 'trick or treat; money or eats.' The woman who had answered the door took time to guess each one's identity.

'He's really enjoying himself,' J.D. said.

'Daniel was so wound up I could hardly get him to eat his supper,' Katie replied, her voice soft. 'He insisted on getting dressed as soon as we got home this afternoon.'

'You did a great job with his costume. It looks so professional.'

'Thanks to the pattern.'

'No, really. You did a good job. Did you make yours, too?'

He saw her nod in the glow of the streetlamp. 'I like to sew. Someday I'd love to make a princess costume.'

He heard the wistful note in her voice. As for himself, he wouldn't mind bringing a little princess on future excursions. 'Maybe you will before long.'

Daniel ran towards them, waving something in his hand. Their thread of conversation dropped. 'I got a candy bar! The good kind, too.'

'So you did,' J.D. declared, knowing 'the good kind' was chocolate and loaded with nuts.

Daniel hurried to the next house, leaving them alone again. J.D. trained the light on his watch. 'We'd better skip a few stops or you won't be home in time.'

'It's OK. I asked Hank to pick me up at your place in case we were running late. I hope you don't mind.'

What could he say? It was one thing to know she was going on a date and another to see her leaving with another man.

'Great,' he said, his voice lacking a heartfelt enthusiasm.

'I'll pick up my car tomorrow,' she said.

'Daniel and I can come by and get you,' J.D. offered, jumping at the ready-made opportunity to find out how her evening had gone. 'How about nine?'

'Good gravy! I'd like a few hours' sleep. Make that eleven and you have a deal.'

The idea of her staying out late with Handsome Hank didn't sit well, but he couldn't object.

'Eleven it is.'

'Oh, look, it's Gwen. You know her. She works in X-Ray.' Suddenly Katie snapped her fingers. 'I should have thought of her sooner. She'd be perfect for you.'

Without giving him a chance to say anything, Katie strode forward to greet the young woman who stood several yards away. Although the night obscured her features, J.D. remembered Gwen as a diminutive brunette who seemed to work long hours, was friendly but not flirtatious and made delicious brownies.

If he hadn't classified Katie as his number one candidate, he might have been tempted. But he had, and so he wasn't.

Feeling like a dog on a leash, J.D. followed and politely acknowledged Gwen. While the two women chatted, J.D. watched for Daniel.

As his son approached, a ninja and a camouflaged soldier of equal size but slighter build ran toward Gwen.

'Come on, Mom,' the two boys declared. 'Hurry up.'

'I'm coming,' Gwen said, the reply sounding automatic. The two raced to the next house without waiting for her, jostling and punching each other on the way.

'Behave yourselves,' she called in a voice lacking any real conviction. The boys, however, didn't pay attention. In the next split second the soldier tripped the ninja and hurried past. The ninja jumped to his feet and raced after his sibling, unconcerned over his dishevelled appearance.

Gwen's sigh was audible. 'Those two are so competitive.'

J.D., who followed at a more sedate pace with Daniel, classified their behaviour as lacking in discipline.

Gwen's boys ran from house to house as if they were setting speed records. By the time the two reached the end of the block near J.D.'s home, J.D. and Daniel were still three stops behind.

Katie and Gwen moved ahead to keep an eye on the boys who were waiting impatiently at the kerb while Daniel and J.D. caught up to them.

'We're going for ice cream before we head for home,' Gwen said. 'Would you like to join us?'

Katie didn't hesitate. 'I can't, but I'm sure J.D. and Daniel would love to go.'

J.D. tried to glower at her, but she smiled brightly and signalled him with a brief nod to accept the other woman's invitation.

He glanced at the two youngsters who fidgeted nearby. Each was liberally covered with crushed leaves and dead grass, as if they'd spent more time fighting than enjoying themselves. On the other hand, the smiles on their faces suggested they *had* been enjoying themselves—perish the thought!

Daniel tugged on his hand. 'I got a coupon for an ice-cream cone in my pumpkin, too. Can we go, Daddy? Please?'

'It's late,' he prevaricated, eyeing the boys who obviously didn't know the meaning of standing still.

Katie broke in. 'Yes, but tomorrow's Saturday. You both can sleep late.'

'Please, Daddy?'

As his biggest argument had been shot full of holes, J.D. couldn't refuse. 'OK,' he said, mentally setting an hour's time limit.

'Gwen's car is down the street,' Katie informed him. 'Your van is right there in the driveway—why don't you take everyone?'

Aware he couldn't refuse without appearing rude, he acquiesced. However, he shot Katie a quelling glance which she seemed to ignore.

'Are you sure you don't mind?' Gwen asked, sounding hesitant. 'We could meet you there.'

'Aw, Mom,' the ninja grumbled. 'We wanna ride in the van. It's cool.'

'I don't mind,' J.D. said, certain he would before the excursion ended. 'Daniel? Take your candy into the house before we leave.'

As Daniel scurried away, a pair of headlights suddenly pinned them in its beam. Moments later, a late-model Corvette pulled to a stop near the kerb and a man in full Kansas City Chiefs football regalia unfolded himself from the inside.

Katie stated the obvious. 'Hank's here. I guess we'll be going.'

Instant jealousy assailed J.D and a totally uncivilised response, much as he'd observed in Gwen's children, filled his soul.

He'd make a point to check out the vehicles her prospective dates drove. How could he compete for her hand when his rivals had impressive trappings of sports cars and no familial responsibilities?

'Have a nice time,' Gwen called out as Katie slowly made her way across the lawn. J.D. echoed her sentiments, although deep down he wished for the opposite.

Daniel bounded to a halt beside J.D. 'Where's Katie goin'? Isn't she coming with us?'

J.D. watched Hank help her into his car. 'No, she's not.'

'But I wanted her to.'

I did, too. 'Maybe next time.' He purposely turned away to face the three children and Gwen. 'Pile in, gang. The ice cream's waiting.'

But for the rest of the evening he couldn't drive away the image of Katie's long Peter Pan legs disappearing inside Hank's car.

Eleven a.m. tomorrow seemed a lifetime away.

CHAPTER SIX

'KATIE'S not home, Daddy.'

J.D. let his arm fall to his side, his knuckles aching from his efforts. After pushing the doorbell for several minutes and pounding for several more, Katie's house remained silent. No running footsteps, no calls, no sounds whatsoever.

The truth glared at him, but he didn't want to admit it. 'Maybe she's still asleep.'

'But Katie never sleeps late,' Daniel protested. 'She told me so herself.'

J.D. didn't answer. He knew Katie's habits well and they matched his own early-bird tendencies. The thought that she might not yet *be* at home rankled him.

Granted, he was early—it was only ten-thirty—but surely she wouldn't still be out. She knew they were coming at eleven.

Although he remembered a few leisurely spent mornings with Ellen, he didn't want to imagine Katie and Handsome Hank indulging in those same activities.

At least the silver Corvette wasn't parked nearby. He was grateful for that.

'Knock again,' he suggested. 'I'll get the key and we'll check inside.' There was always the possibility that she was ill and unable to answer the door. Granted, he was clutching at the flimsiest excuse, but a feeble one was better than the alternative.

Red lava rock surrounded the foundation of her bungalow and served as the backdrop for a ceramic bird bath, several rabbits and frogs. While he didn't agree with her methods, her trick of leaving her key in plain sight occasionally came in handy.

He lifted a large, satisfied-looking frog off a large rock, reached inside its mouth and retrieved a duplicate of her house key. In the blink of an eye he replaced the frog in its place.

'We're in business now,' he told Daniel as he bent over to insert the key in the hole.

'Look! She's coming!'

J.D. glanced in the direction Daniel was pointing and saw Katie walking towards them from a stone's throw away. She was wearing a pair of tight-fitting, stone-washed jeans and a long-sleeved purple sweater. The long strap of her oversized bag hung over one shoulder.

Daniel waved and she returned the gesture. 'Am I late?' she asked as she approached.

J.D. noticed her slow gait but his distress over her whereabouts manifested itself before he could control it. 'Where have you been? I was getting worried.'

Katie looked surprised by his concern. 'Is it past eleven already? I thought I'd be back in plenty of time.'

'That's OK,' Daniel piped up. 'We're early. We was gonna go inside 'cause Daddy thought you might be sick and couldn't hear us knocking.'

'How thoughtful of you,' she told Daniel.

J.D. thrust the key in his son's hand. 'Would you put this back for me, please?'

Daniel scampered down the three porch steps and went straight for the frog.

'Your leg's sore today, isn't it?' J.D. asked.

Katie opened the door. 'Yesterday was a little hard on my knee, but I'll survive.'

'Why didn't he give you a chair?' J.D. knew how long it took to work the kinks out of her muscles when she grew overtired and his indignation on her behalf escalated.

'I didn't ask because I didn't want anyone making a fuss.' Her expression became intent. 'Were you really worried about me…or just afraid I hadn't come home yet?'

Realising she'd seen right through him, he grinned sheepishly. 'Both.'

'I'm a big girl, you know.'

Studying her form, he noticed the tanned skin revealed by the V-neckline of her form-fitting sweater and the distinctive shape of unfettered breasts. When had she started going *au naturel*?

Having a new hairdo to attract a man's eye, that was one thing; revealing her physical assets, that was quite another. He didn't know what kind of fibre the manufacturer had used to create her sweater, but the texture appeared as soft and fuzzy as a kitten's fur. His hands itched to find out for himself.

Good thing she hadn't worn this on her date last night.

'I know,' he said hoarsely. He cleared his throat and hoped he wouldn't sound like an overprotective parent. 'So where have you been?'

'I ran out of toothpaste, so I ran—walked, actually—to the Cosy Corner and bought a tube. See?' She dug in the voluminous bag which contained everything from A to Z and withdrew a distinctive red and white rectangular box.

She brandished her purchase like a schoolteacher's chiding finger. 'Now don't you feel ridiculous for thinking such naughty thoughts?'

His face warmed. 'It was possible,' he defended himself.

She quirked one eyebrow at him. 'Daniel?' she called, pinning J.D. like a Monarch butterfly to a display board with her gaze. 'Would you like to ride your tricycle on the patio for a while?'

Daniel shot through the kitchen and into the back yard like greased lightning. As soon as the wooden screen door slammed behind him, J.D. felt Katie's wrath.

'What kind of person do you think I am?' she demanded. 'I don't sleep around, much less with someone on the first date. Nor do I intend to start now, even if I *am* looking for a husband. I'm surprised you let me look after Daniel if you think I'm so lacking in character.'

J.D. held up his hands in surrender. 'I didn't mean that at all.'

She planted both hands on her hips. 'Then what *did* you mean?'

'Being a guy, I know the tricks…'

'Ah, so you're an expert in this area? Or are you describing the grand finale of your own dates?'

'Absolutely not,' he said. 'I've been in enough locker rooms to know the pressure tactics some guys will use to get what they want. That's all.'

'You obviously don't have a very high opinion of me or of Hank, do you?'

A minefield couldn't have been more dangerous.

He chose his words carefully. 'I don't know the man well enough one way or the other. If you recall, I didn't recommend him.'

'For your information, Hank was the perfect gentleman. We went to his friends' party and had a great time. He had to go on duty at six this morning so he brought me home around one last night. Now, if you'll excuse me, I have to brush my teeth.'

She limped towards the bathroom, her shoulders high.

J.D. berated himself for his tactless handling of the situation. He had loads of faith in Katie, but Hank was the unknown variable in the equation. Playboys came in all shapes and sizes…and professions.

If she'd dropped her important titbit of information about Hank having an early shift, J.D. wouldn't have fretted and stewed for most of the night.

She returned five minutes later, wearing a pair of low-riding black jogging pants and a white T-shirt that read NURSES CALL THE SHOTS.

He tried to make amends. 'So you had a great time.'

'Yes, I did.' Her tone held traces of belligerence as she sank onto the sofa and stretched out her sore leg.

He sat at the far end and motioned for her to put her foot in his lap. She complied and he began massaging the knotted muscles.

'Perfect,' she murmured as her leg relaxed under his hands. 'You should have been a masseur.'

'If I ever give up medicine, I'll consider it,' he said. 'Are you going out with hands…er…Hank again?'

'I don't know. Why?'

He shrugged, pretending her decision didn't matter. 'If you're interested in him then I won't send any more eligible fellows your way.'

She fell silent. 'Hank is a nice guy and I enjoy being with him, but…'

'But?' he prompted, wishing he didn't have fabric lying between his fingers and her skin.

Katie ran her hands through her hair. 'He kissed me, but there wasn't any magic.'

'No chemistry?'

She shook her head. 'Not enough to mention. Maybe I just need more practice.'

He tried not to think about her kissing anyone other than himself. 'He's not the only fish in the sea.'

'Yeah, but the numbers are certainly dwindling. The good ones are already married and those who are left are still single for good reason. Hey, I thought you didn't appreciate fish references.'

He gave her a sheepish grin. 'It seemed appropriate.'

Her face brightened. 'Speaking of fish, I want to hear how things went with Gwen.'

'Gwen and her gorillas, you mean.'

Katie giggled. 'It couldn't have been that bad.'

He quirked one eyebrow. 'Oh, yeah? Have you spent any time with her two terrors?'

'No.'

'Then I rest my case. Were you aware that her kids aren't twins?'

'Yes. They're a year apart.'

'Well, I thought they were twins. Boys, in fact. I

was quite surprised when the ninja took off his head-gear and he was really a girl.'

'Didn't I tell you their names? Morgan and Taylor.'

'Even if you had, I wouldn't have known,' he said dryly. 'Their names aren't a good clue. Why can't people pick names that don't leave you guessing if their kid is a boy or a girl?'

'Everyone wants their son or daughter to be different, I suppose.' She settled against the cushions. 'You can stop now. My leg's feeling better.'

Reluctantly, he obeyed.

'So tell me what happened,' she said. 'I'm all ears.'

J.D. settled against the cushions. 'Other than squabbling the entire time, spilling their soda pop at the table or dropping a half-eaten cone in my lap? Not much. I think the manager counted the minutes until we left.'

'Over-exuberant kids,' she said, sounding unconcerned. 'Gwen is OK, wouldn't you agree?'

How could he admit to spending the whole hour comparing her to Katie? Or deciding that Gwen had fallen short?

'She's a nice person,' he said slowly, 'but I want a wife who won't let her kids—*our* kids—run roughshod over her. Life with the Dangerous Duo would be utter chaos. I'd either be in jail for child abuse or I'd have to enroll them in the nearest military boarding school.'

'But you're so patient with kids. I can't believe you'd resort to such things.'

'There's a difference between potential juvenile delinquents and sick children.' He grinned. 'Now that I think about it, I'd like a wife who can make a hardened criminal quake in his boots.'

She swatted him playfully. 'You won't ever let me forget that incident, will you?'

'Not a chance.' He changed the subject. 'Some of the guys and I are going to play football this afternoon at the park. Want to come along?'

She frowned as she rubbed her knee. 'I should spend the afternoon reviewing the EMS manual.'

'Bring it along,' he said, trying to hide how anxious he was for her to agree. Then, playing on her sympathies most shamelessly, he added, 'Daniel missed having you go with us for ice cream last night. He'll be really disappointed if you don't join us today. I'll bring a blanket and you can stretch out under a tree.'

'OK.'

He rose. 'Let's go.'

She appeared shocked. 'Now?'

J.D. put on his most hangdog expression. 'I've been trying to rake leaves this morning, but with Daniel around it was a lost cause. His idea of helping is to jump in the piles.'

He could have managed quite easily, but he wanted to include Katie in their activities. Usually he kept Daniel all to himself on the weekends, but now he intended to change their routine. The days of passing each other like ships in the night, with an occasional stop in port for a meal or to study, were over.

Without giving her time to object, J.D. summoned Daniel and bustled her out the door. He opened the passenger side of the van and held out his hand to assist her inside.

She hesitated, as if unsure of what to do. He regretted his lapse in showing her such courtesies.

'What's the occasion for such royal treatment?'

'Humour me,' he said, putting his hand under her elbow to give her a small boost. Then, because he sensed the truth would make her uncomfortable, he told a white lie.

'I don't want to undo the hard work I put in on your knee.'

To J.D.'s delight, she accepted his help without further argument.

Once they'd arrived at his house, he brought out a lawn chair and parked it on the driveway. 'Your throne, my lady.'

'I can help,' she protested.

J.D. shook his head. 'Sorry. Us guys don't want to share the fun. Right, Daniel?'

'Right, Daddy.' Daniel ran to the garage and returned with a child-sized rake. 'Watch me, Katie.'

Katie sat down. 'I'm watching.'

J.D. began creating a pile of leaves with Daniel's help. As soon as it stood as high as Daniel's waist, Daniel threw down his rake. 'Can I jump in now?'

'I'm trying to put these in a bag,' J.D. reminded him. 'We talked about this earlier.'

'I know, but Katie hasn't seen me jump in,' Daniel said. 'Please?'

'Do you promise this is the last time?' J.D. asked.

Daniel's head bobbed up and down, his hazel eyes intent. 'I promise.'

'I guess if this is the last time I'd better make it bigger.'

'OK, Daddy.'

Before long, the mound of leaves stood as tall as

Daniel. Elated, he ran into the garage and returned a few minutes later, carrying a five-gallon bucket. 'Is it ready now?'

J.D. smiled, guessing his son's plan. 'It's ready.'

Daniel turned the container upside down and scrambled on top. 'Watch me, Katie.'

'I'm watching,' she reassured him.

Daniel held out his arms and made aeroplane noises. In the next instant he jumped right in the middle of the heap, scattering leaves everywhere.

An instant later he poked his head out of the much smaller pile. 'Did you see me?' he demanded.

'You were wonderful,' Katie declared, brushing off the leaves that had landed on her clothes.

'Can I do it again?'

Katie rose. 'Why don't we find something for lunch while Daddy finishes his chores?'

'I'm not hungry.'

She held out her hand. 'No, but I am. Besides, I haven't seen all the candy you brought home last night. Did you get any of my favourite?'

The leaves effectively forgotten in favour of sweets, Daniel followed Katie into the house, chattering about the treats he'd received.

Katie certainly had a way with Daniel, J.D. thought as he quickly stuffed the leaves into garbage sacks and placed them on the kerb. He doubted if anyone else would build the same rapport with his son. Then again, it wasn't surprising. For all intents and purposes, Katie had acted as his mother from early on.

Once again he berated himself for not thinking of Katie as a prospective wife before now. It would be so much simpler if he just announced his intentions.

Yet his plan to stack the proverbial deck in his favour was a good one. With luck and careful engineering, he was bound to come out ahead in the final tally.

His only problem would be if she surprised him by seriously considering those other prospects. If so, he wasn't disinclined to point out their obvious faults.

Ideas on how to accomplish his goal raced through his mind even as they joined a growing contingent of friends for an afternoon at the park. Most of them were ER staff—Michael and his wife Elaine; Marty, the middle-aged, balding physician's assistant, and his wife, Nancy; Lee and his girlfriend; and a few other Mercer staff members.

Michael's eldest daughter, a responsible thirteen-year-old, was placed in charge of the children so the parents could play ball.

'We're one person short,' Michael told J.D and Katie as they spread a blanket out under a tree. 'Julio had a make-up soccer game and will come as soon as he's finished. Elaine isn't in any condition to play so she's going to referee and act as timekeeper.'

With Elaine being five months pregnant, J.D. agreed.

'Katie,' Michael continued, 'Would you fill in until a replacement arrives?'

'I don't think—' J.D. began.

Katie interrupted. 'What do I have to do?'

What was the woman thinking? If she struggled to walk after standing all day, how would she move if she tried to run? Someone had to be the voice of reason.

J.D. tried again. 'Your knee—'

She glared at him. 'Is fine.' Turning toward Michael, she asked, 'Where do you want me?'

'You can be quarterback,' Michael said. 'I'll pass the ball to you and all you have to do is throw it to whoever's open to receive.'

'No tackling?'

He handed her a large red man's handkerchief to tuck in the back waistband of her pants. 'No tackling. This is *flag* football.'

'You're forgetting that I've heard stories about how you guys play, including detailed accounts of every ache and pain. Or were those exaggerations?'

Michael gave her a boyish grin. 'We have to brag about how rough and tough we are. But don't worry. No one can get to you unless they go through me first.'

She eyed his bulk and J.D. could see her mind mulling over the situation. 'You've got yourself a quarterback.'

'Good. You're on my team,' Michael said. 'OK, everybody, line up.'

J.D. pulled her aside. 'This isn't a good idea.'

'Maybe not, but it's my choice.' She smiled sweetly. 'See you at the goal line.'

As Katie had never joined them before, J.D. hadn't ever given any thought to the way spouses were placed on opposite teams. This time, however, he immediately saw the advantage. Husband guarded wife and if a couple indulged in a little extracurricular kissing or illegal holding, no one objected.

The idea of grabbing Katie in the interests of the game and with the team's full blessing was charged with potential. He positioned himself on the scrimmage line ready to take advantage of every possible opportunity.

'I don't like that gleam in your eye,' she told him as she took the quarterback's position behind the centre player.

J.D. gave her a feral grin. 'What gleam?'

'That one.'

'Just getting into the spirit of the game.'

Elaine blew the whistle and the game began. J.D. was impressed with how well Katie did. She caught the football without fumbling and always managed to throw it to a receiver before he could get past Michael.

At the start of the second quarter, Katie made her first fumble as she caught the ball. J.D. feinted left, then moved right past Michael. He caught Katie in a massive bear hug, but someone pushed him from behind and he found himself falling.

Conscious of Katie's weak leg, he twisted his body so as not to drop on top of her. He landed hard on his back but the feel of Katie's hips nestled against his lower half and her chest pressed against his torso gave him an entirely new ache—one not to be soothed by a topical ointment.

Her face hovered a mere inch from his, her mouth within easy kissing distance.

His body strained against the zipper of his ancient blue jeans and every nerve ending seemed to quiver in anticipation. Heat suffused his skin until he thought he'd have to remove his grey sweatshirt or combust.

'Are you OK?' he asked, conscious of her breath dancing across his cheek.

'Yeah.'

He stared at her mouth, wanting to taste her in a slow, knock-her-socks-off fashion. 'You're sure?'

'Absolutely. What about you?'

'I'm fine. Just great.' And he was. What a shame they had an audience.

'Hey, you two, quit wasting game time,' Michael complained.

J.D. planted a quick, feather-light kiss on her lips, wishing he could take more time and far greater care. Now, however, wasn't the place. Willing his body to dormancy, he jumped to his feet and helped an obviously dazed Katie do the same.

Michael came over to study her. 'Are you sure you're OK?'

'Yeah. I'm fine.'

The breathless quality to her voice brought a smile to J.D.'s face. If such a brief, platonic peck could reduce Katie to befuddlement, what would a serious kiss do to her?

He planned to find out.

After his initial tackle, he made contact with Katie often. Even after she'd thrown the ball to one of her team's receivers and was no longer involved in the play, he made a point to chase after her, enjoying the sight of her *derrière* before he grabbed her.

The whisper of her breath against his face, the feel of her pressed against his body, the scent of her in his nostrils and the sound of her laughter in his ears, made him wish the game would last for ever.

But all good things came to an end and after he'd managed to gently bring her down to the ground for the third time he saw a flash of pain steal across her face.

'I think it's time to quit,' she said. Her voice was shaky and her face pale.

Remorse filled him and he jumped to his feet. 'Did I hurt you? I didn't mean to—'

'No, I'm not hurt. My knee is aching a little bit. That's all.'

'That's all? That's plenty!' he exploded. 'Why didn't you say something sooner?' He turned to the group and yelled, 'Time out!' Then he helped her limp towards the sidelines where they'd placed several lawn chairs.

'It didn't hurt until now. Please, don't make a fuss. A little rest and I'll be as good as new.' She managed a chuckle. 'Too bad my new look didn't include a new knee.'

He whipped the white hanky out of his hip pocket, wrapped several cubes of ice from the drink chest in it, then placed his makeshift cold pack on her knee. 'This should help.'

'Thanks. I'm sorry I didn't last the whole game.'

'You shouldn't have been playing at all,' he said sternly, 'so don't worry about not finishing.' A shout drew his attention and he glanced up to see Julio approaching with his family.

'Replacements have arrived so you sit there and cheer for the white team.' He grinned.

'And be a traitor to the red?' she asked, her horror obviously feigned. 'No way.'

In spite of her avowal of loyalty to her teammates, J.D. heard her cheer whenever he made a good play or intercepted the ball. Although Julio wasn't as much fun to guard as Katie had been, knowing she was rooting for him made up for her absence on the field.

Later, as they drove home, Daniel asked, 'Did you have fun, Katie?'

'Yes, I did, short stuff,' she said.

'Wanna come with us next time?'

'Sure. If I'm not working.'

Daniel addressed J.D. 'Did *you* have a good time, Daddy?'

J.D. exchanged a smile with Katie. 'Yes, I did.'

'I did, too,' Daniel declared. 'How come when you grown-ups play, everybody kisses everybody else? They don't do that on TV.'

J.D. was momentarily at a loss for words.

'Is it because you're all mommies and daddies?'

'That's right,' J.D. answered, hoping Katie would mull over his son's comment. To his relief, he pulled to a stop in front of Katie's house before Daniel could voice any more observations.

'I'll be right back,' he told Daniel before he slipped out of the van to walk Katie to her door. He didn't want his conversation overheard by little ears.

'Don't forget my programme next Sunday,' Daniel called out. 'Not tomorrow, but the next one.'

'I won't,' Katie promised as she joined J.D. on the sidewalk.

J.D. slowed his stride to match hers. 'Thanks for going with us today. I hope you won't suffer any after-effects from all the physical activity.'

'A long soak in the tub and I'll be good as new.' She hesitated near the bottom step. 'I've been thinking about what happened today. People will think you and I have something going when we don't. It's bound to make it harder to find you a wife.'

He hadn't thought of it before but, now that she'd

mentioned it, gossip about this afternoon could work to his advantage. 'Really?'

'Yes. And to counteract any rumours, I've come up with someone else you should meet.'

J.D. didn't want to meet anyone else. In his own mind, he'd already found the perfect candidate.

'I'm not sure about our plan,' he said slowly. 'Maybe I'm rushing things.'

'What about convincing the board you're going to stay? Don't you want a wife any more?'

'Yes, but I'm not having very good luck with this dating thing. I could use some pointers on what women expect these days before I take another plunge.'

She nibbled on her bottom lip and he pressed on. This time he used a teasing tone in order to test her reaction. 'It would be easier if we just tied the knot.'

Her jaw dropped. 'You're not serious, are you?'

He shrugged, pretending nonchalance. 'We get along well. In fact, we probably know each other better than most couples do when they get married.'

'We probably do,' she agreed, 'but the adage "familiarity breeds contempt" was coined for a reason. I have much more faith in our lists. This way we'll both find the spouse we really want.'

'We haven't done very well so far,' he reminded her. 'In fact, I'd describe our dates so far as disasters.' He silently added the word 'fortuitous'.

She pressed her mouth into a thoughtful line. 'Maybe our specifications could use a little fine-tuning.'

'I think you're right.' He didn't mention how he thought his required a complete overhaul.

'We can work on it after Daniel's programme,'

he added, mentally pledging to redouble his efforts towards showing her how well they fitted each other.

'That's nearly a week away.'

'Then how about this Monday or Tuesday?'

'OK, but I still think you should call—'

'I'd rather wait,' he said firmly. 'It's time to regroup. After that…we'll see.'

She heaved a resigned sigh. 'I suppose it would be for the best.'

J.D. mentally rubbed his hands together as he anticipated carrying out his new plan. In the meantime, he intended to tailor his new list to fit Katie Alexander right down to the sprinkle of freckles across her nose.

CHAPTER SEVEN

THE first week of November ended on a cold and wet note, bringing an end to the last few days of Indian summer. The change in temperature and rain brought a sudden influx of sniffles and sore throats to the ER, including a host of elderly people who'd slipped on slick sidewalks and pavement.

On Friday afternoon, J.D. had finished reviewing the positive strep screen results on two-year-old Richie Moses and was writing orders for an antibiotic when the telephone rang. Ashley snatched it off its cradle to answer it.

She listened intently for a few seconds. 'I don't think we can,' she said apologetically. 'Hospital policy says we can't treat anyone unless they come into the ER. The front entrance doesn't qualify. You'll have to call an ambulance.'

His interest aroused, J.D. interrupted. 'What's wrong?'

Ashley cupped her hand over the mouthpiece. 'A man in his early twenties collapsed on the lawn. The receptionist says he's bleeding and wants to know if we can send someone to get him.'

The word 'bleeding' captured J.D.'s attention. 'Absolutely.'

'But what about the policy?'

He wished Katie was on duty. She wouldn't have questioned his decision. Come to think of it, she probably would have sent help without consulting him in the first place.

'To hell with the policy,' he stated, rising. 'This man is in need of assistance. We can sort through the technicalities later.'

Ashley stared at him, her eyes wide with fear over the breach of protocol. 'Are you sure you don't want an ambulance?'

He didn't waste time on giving an answer. Instead, he commandeered Marty and a part-time nurse named June, briefing them on the situation.

While they hurried away to load the gurney with basic supplies, J.D. faced Ashley and spoke succinctly. 'How many ambulances does Mercer have?'

'Two.'

'You've been listening to the same radio channels I have. Where are those two units?'

She had the grace to look sheepish. 'One's at the school, dealing with an insulin reaction. The other's at the nursing home.'

'Exactly. And by the time they get around to us, our injured man could bleed to death. How do you think the reputation of Mercer Memorial will fare when word leaks out about how we let a man die on the front lawn?'

At that moment Marty reappeared in his yellow protective gown so J.D. didn't wait for Ashley's response. He caught the pair of latex gloves which the physician's assistant had tossed him and tugged them on. Rushing out of ER, he mentally steeled himself for what he might encounter.

In truth, he wasn't sure how his breach of protocol would go over with the legal beagles, but he had sworn the Hippocratic oath and no pencil-pushing, policy-making businessman or lawyer would make him disregard his solemn vow.

He tore through the hospital corridors, leaving his assistants to bring up the rear. In the lobby a security guard, who looked too young for his position, held the assembled crowd of people in check as they all craned their necks for the best view of the excitement.

'Move aside,' J.D. announced. The crowd parted down the middle and allowed him access, but the people didn't disperse. It was as if each person had the opportunity to see a live episode of *ER* and none wanted to miss out on the drama. 'Call the police.'

Without waiting to see who obeyed his order, he rushed outside. The rumble of the gurney's wheels against the sidewalk told him of his team's nearby presence.

The man lay just off the sidewalk, clearly having tried to reach help but collapsing a few short steps from his goal. Blood saturated his clothing and the grass around him.

J.D. knelt at his side, immediately assessing multiple stab wounds in the upper left abdominal quadrant. The skin covering both sides of his ribs was purple, as if someone had used him as a punching bag. Possible liver and spleen damage were his immediate diagnoses.

He glanced at the man's face, guessing him to be about twenty. His hair was long, his moustache neatly trimmed. Dirt streaked his jeans and sleeveless T-shirt, and grease stained his fingernail beds and hands. A snake tattoo covered a muscular biceps.

'Put some pressure on these,' J.D. said, indicating the puncture marks. 'Let's get him inside, stat.'

As soon as the bandages were in place, J.D. helped his team hoist the man on the gurney. Moments later he was strapped in and headed for a trauma room.

Once there, J.D. spouted orders in rapid-fire succession. 'Start two IVs with large-bore needles. I want an airway. Notify Surgery we're sending him up as soon as he's stable.

'Get a CBC, crossmatch for four units, electrolytes, coag studies, drug screen—'

'BP is falling,' June said. 'Pulse is increased.'

Time stood still while J.D. worked frantically to reverse the man's hypovolaemic shock. Unwilling to wait for a lab tech to arrive, he instructed Marty to draw the blood samples and send the specimens to the stat lab. Before long the report came back—the haemoglobin had reached critically low values.

Dr Li, one of the surgeons, arrived and whistled as he peered over J.D.'s shoulder. 'Spleen and liver,' he said.

'My thoughts exactly,' J.D. replied.

'Pat's nearly finished,' Dr Li said, referring to his other surgical colleague. 'I'll have him scrub with me. Send our John Doe up as soon as you can.' With that, the diminutive Chinese-American physician disappeared.

J.D. knew this man's survival depended on replacing the lost fluids. If he failed, Mr Doe would never see the inside of an operating room. 'Is the blood ready yet?'

'It will be in a few minutes,' June reported.

'Hang two units and get him up to Surgery,' J.D. said, anxious to send this man upstairs to a suite where they could repair the damage.

J.D. hoped and prayed that this would not turn into a coroner's case.

'Do we have a name yet?' Marty asked.

Heads shook.

Ashley appeared in the doorway. 'The boy from the school is on his way. ETA is five minutes.'

'Call the paediatrician to cover,' J.D. said. 'I saw him earlier. He might still be in the building.' J.D. wasn't about to leave his current patient—his condition was far too precarious.

'I lost the pulse,' June announced calmly.

Someone wheeled the crash cart alongside the gurney. J.D. grabbed the paddles and Marty squirted enough paste to cover their smooth surfaces.

'Clear,' J.D. called out as he positioned the defibrillator paddles on the man's chest.

Electricity jolted through the man's body, but the flat line EKG remained unchanged.

'Three hundred,' J.D. said, instructing Marty to increase the voltage. Once again he repeated the procedure.

The monitor's horizontal line was ominous.

'Three-sixty.'

The room's occupants waited for results that never came.

He held out his hand. 'Epinephrine.'

June slapped a syringe with a long needle into his hand. Without hesitation, J.D. plunged it into John Doe's heart.

But the results remained the same—the small blip on the screen continued on its straight path.

J.D. had lost the battle.

Feeling old beyond his years, he straightened.

'That's it,' he said wearily. 'Time of death is fifteen-oh-eight.'

The team froze for a few seconds, as if paying their respects to the man on the gurney. June silently began disconnecting monitors and IV lines from the equipment they'd used.

Everything they'd inserted into his body—the endotrach tube and the catheters—remained in place. Due to the nature of Mr Doe's injuries, there would be an autopsy and John Doe's death classified as a homicide.

J.D. stripped off his bloodied gloves, the soiled gown and goggles, threw the items into the trash, then strode from the room. Others would deal with taking the body to the morgue; phone calls and paperwork were his responsibility.

Officer Giles intercepted him as he rounded the corner. 'How's he doing?'

J.D. shook his head. 'We couldn't save him. Massive blood loss, cardiac arrest.'

'We found an abandoned car a few blocks away, registered to a Rex Pollard. We're trying to locate his whereabouts or find a family member to ID him.'

'He has a cobra tattooed on his left bicep. I didn't see anything else.'

Hank scribbled a note on his pad. 'Sounds like Rex. Did he say anything? Mention who'd attacked him?'

J.D. shook his head. 'He was unconscious the whole time.'

'Too bad. It's probably a drug deal gone bad. For someone coming from a law-abiding family, Rex wasn't known to be a model citizen.'

Giles disappeared. By the time J.D. had notified

the coroner, the hallway had suddenly become a beehive of activity.

Several staff members wheeled the young diabetic boy out of their trauma room towards the elevators. Katie, wearing her EMT uniform, spoke to her partner, Doug, then strode towards J.D..

'How did it go?' she asked.

'We lost him.'

'I'm sorry.'

'So am I.' He rubbed his forehead. 'The police are looking for a family member to positively identify the body. I feel like I've failed.'

'You didn't fail. You did your best,' she reminded him. 'That's all anyone can expect. The human body can only take so much trauma. I heard you found him on the lawn.'

'News travels fast.'

'Of course. This was the most exciting thing to happen here since Surgery had a gas leak. You're a regular hero.'

'Hardly,' he said, thinking of the body lying on a slab in the morgue. Even if Rex Pollard hadn't lived a noble life, he didn't deserve such an ignominious death.

He forced his thoughts elsewhere. 'How was your run?'

'Not as exciting as yours. By the time we got there the teacher had already given him his emergency injection. Apparently our little fellow had been drowsy and nauseous all morning so his teacher kept a close eye on him. Dr Shannon suspects that his insulin dosage needs some adjustment to compensate for his growth spurt. He's admitting him until he's stabilised.'

'At least we've had one happy ending.'

'There will be more,' she said.

'You're right,' he said, struggling to regain his perspective. Losing a patient, it was never easy. It reminded him of his own limitations and of how their technological advances still hadn't solved all the problems confronting the human body. His job would be simpler if weapons and tempers didn't mix.

He changed the subject. 'Will you be back tomorrow?'

She grinned. 'Miss me already?'

If she only knew how much...He faked a mournful expression. 'No one's here to make decent coffee. My day is ruined before it begins.'

She clucked her tongue. 'Haven't you followed the directions I posted?'

'Yeah, but it doesn't taste the same.'

'Poor thing,' she said, her down-in-the-mouth sympathy clearly artificial. 'But I'll take pity on you and make sure there's a pot ready early in the morning. Hey, weren't you supposed to hear from the board today?'

He glanced at the clock. The hours had slipped by, but he'd had good reason for his absence. 'Actually, I'd planned to attend the meeting, but fate intervened. I'll sneak up now and find out what they decided.'

After the afternoon he'd had, surely the odds of hearing positive news were in his favour.

'I can't believe the board is dragging its feet,' J.D. told Katie later that evening. Daniel was in bed for the night and J.D. felt like a clock wound too tight. Unable to sit still, he paced the living room.

'Did they say why?'

'They have to study the feasibility. Can you believe it? What's to study? I have everything outlined—the cost projections, the floor plans, it's all there.'

'Maybe your document was too daunting and they haven't had a chance to read it.'

'They received it three weeks ago. How much longer do they need?'

She smiled. 'They could have just said no to start with. Be grateful they didn't.'

'I know. I want this project to go through so badly…'

'It will. Be patient. They'll come around to your way of thinking. Wait and see.' She patted the sofa beside her. 'Now, stop acting like a caged tiger and relax.'

He sat. 'You're very confident.'

'You have a fabulous idea. Given the chance, our board will see it, too.'

J.D. stared at her for a moment. 'You really are an optimistic person, aren't you?'

She grinned. 'It beats being the opposite.'

'Were you always Suzy Sunshine? Even as a kid?'

Katie grabbed a decorator pillow and threw it at him.

He caught it. 'Hey, what did I do?'

'I *hate* that name. I hated it as a child and I haven't altered my opinion.'

'Ah,' he said knowingly. 'So you always were cheerful like this.'

'I guess. I thought I was being normal until I realised how many people look on the bad side of things. My mother always told me that whining and complaining didn't do anything except give you wrinkles.'

J.D. leaned closer to stare into her face. Her smooth skin begged to be touched and he indulged himself. 'Wise woman, your mother. Not a wrinkle in sight. She must have been remarkable.'

Katie didn't seem startled by his actions, a fact he found encouraging. 'She was. After she died of cancer, I moved in with Gideon and took care of things for him.'

No wonder she had such a fully developed mothering instinct. 'Kept him on the straight and narrow, I'll bet.'

'Absolutely. Now his wife has the dubious honour.' She yawned. 'Sorry. I didn't realise I was tired until a few minutes ago.'

'That's what comes from burning the candle at both ends.'

'If you're going to start in about my ambulance job, I'm going home.'

'No, I'm not. Just stating the obvious. How's the knee, by the way?'

'It's fine.'

'No problems with lifting or carrying?'

'Not one. I couldn't ask for a better partner than Doug.' A soft smile appeared on her mouth. 'He's absolutely wonderful to work with. All the guys are.'

'Absolutely wonderful' wasn't what J.D. wanted to hear. 'Are there any other women on the payroll?'

'No.' She grinned. 'I guess that's why they give me the red-carpet treatment.'

'I would think the wives aren't too happy.'

'Only two of the fellows are married and both of them are in their fifties,' she said. 'The others are single.'

More competition, he thought to himself.

'Any of them good prospects?' he asked, waiting with bated breath for her reply. If so, he wanted to know who he was up against.

'It's really too soon to tell,' she said. 'And speaking of prospects, we should work on your list.'

'We don't have to, you know.' The more she focused on him, the better his chances of success.

She stared at him as if a tumour had sprouted on his face. 'We've been together every night this week and haven't worked on it once. Every time I've brought up the subject, you've said, "Later." The longer you put this off, the longer it will be until you find your future wife.'

'OK.' He pulled a small square of yellow paper out of his pocket. 'Here's my new list.'

Katie unfolded the page until it grew to legal-tablet size. 'Good heavens! When did you come up with this?'

'This week. Off and on.' He'd taken advantage of their time together during the past few days to record his impressions of Katie.

She read a few of the points. '"Optimistic, easy-going. Willing to try new things. Freckles."' She stared at him. 'Freckles? What has that got to do with anything?'

He shrugged. 'It's *my* list for *my* dream wife and

I want freckles. If you can ask for blue eyes, I can request freckles.'

'If you recall, I scratched off blue eyes.'

'OK, but I still want freckles.'

A dubious expression covered her face. 'Number eighteen says "mutual physical attraction". How am I supposed to decide that?'

'You aren't. It's one of the criteria I have to screen for myself. It goes hand in hand with wanting more children. Can't get kids without sex and if she doesn't appeal to me, it's impossible to—'

Her face turned pink. 'I get the picture.' She ran her finger down the list. '"Number nineteen. A soul mate."'

'Someone I can talk to.' He grinned. 'We're not going to spend all of our time between the sheets.'

Picturing Katie in his bed, that took very little effort—she was an attractive woman. He simply had to convince her that she belonged there.

'Why the frown?' he asked.

'Are you sure about the freckles?'

'Absolutely. Why?'

'You're being unrealistic. The only way I could come up with someone like this is to genetically engineer her. And by the time technology does that, you'll be too old to want a wife.'

'I'm not worried. I'm sure you'll think of someone.' Surely she would deduce the identity of the one person who was made to order—herself.

'What about your previous list? Does this one cancel out the other?'

He pointed to the yellow page in her hand. 'Go by this one. As for you,' he continued, 'I ran into someone you'll like—Francis Ostmeyer.'

'Francis?'

'Yeah. He's the roofer I hired last spring to fix the leak. He's the F in B&F Roofers.'

'Oh. How nice.'

'You said you wanted a manual labourer,' he reminded her. 'Francis is a real likes-to-get-his-hands-dirty kind of guy. So when he contacts you don't be surprised.'

'Do people really call him Francis?'

'He prefers Frankie.'

'I suppose that is an improvement.'

'Francis isn't so bad,' he protested.

'No, but I'll bet the kids teased him mercilessly.'

'I'm sure they didn't do it for long. Frankie was a wrestler in high school. State champion for several years, according to the plaques in his office. With your swimming records, you two should have a lot to talk about.'

In fact, Frankie's previous accomplishments were *all* he talked about.

She hid a yawn behind her hand. 'If you say so.'

Watching her lean her head against the cushions and close her eyes, he smiled. 'You really should go to bed.'

'I will. Just as soon as I can get off the sofa.' She didn't move.

He paused, listening to her gentle breathing while watching the rise and fall of her chest. 'Katie?'

'Hmm?'

'You're not in any shape to drive home.'

'Sure I am,' she said, her eyes still closed. 'I'm resting my eyelids for a few minutes.'

'Why don't you spend the night? The spare room is ready.'

In his mind it belonged to Katie. His parents used it when they paid him a visit, but of all his guests Katie slept there the most often. The arrangement was ideal for those nights when she looked after Daniel while he covered Michael's shift or worked a twenty-four-hour weekend stint.

'Sounds good,' she mumbled.

He waited for her to move, but she didn't. 'Would you like me to carry you?' he finally asked, hoping she wouldn't respond. He'd like to carry her to bed, preferably *his*.

Patience, he told himself.

As he turned down the blankets, he remembered when the three of them had picked out the curtains and bedspread. They had pored over the home interior section of the J.C. Penney's catalogue, trying to find a design and colour agreeable to everyone.

Daniel, of course, had wanted a Nascar racing bedspread with matching checkerboard draperies. J.D. had wanted something unisex because he didn't enjoy sleeping in feminine frills and wouldn't subject his father or any other male to such a fate.

In the end, Kate had suggested a compromise. Daniel got the Nascar comforter for his bed and J.D.'s guest room sported a blue-and-rose-coloured plaid quilt.

He returned to find her burrowed deeper into the cushions. 'Come on, Sleeping Beauty,' he murmured. 'Let's get you to beddy-bye.'

Sliding his hands under her hips and behind her back, he lifted her easily.

She made a low sound in her throat, almost like a kitten's purr. Too bad only a few yards separated him from his destination.

He placed her on the mattress and slid off her shoes. After a few minutes of inner debate, he unfastened her jeans and removed those as well, discovering a pair of white lacy underpants in the process.

He grinned. Had she always preferred such feminine attire, or had that come about as part of her make-over? Someday he hoped to have his question answered.

Although he imagined it uncomfortable to sleep in a bra, he wasn't about to test her good nature by removing it. Instead, he slipped his hands underneath her back and unhooked the clasp, trying not to notice the soft warmth of her skin and failing miserably.

He covered her with the blanket, noticing how her knee didn't appear to have suffered any lasting consequences from their football game. With a sigh of relief he laid his guilty feelings to rest.

As he closed the door on his way out, he realised how much he enjoyed having her under his roof. Now, if only he could turn it into a permanent arrangement.

On Saturday morning, J.D. placed a plate of crisp, microwaved bacon on the table moments before Katie entered the kitchen dressed in yesterday's clothes.

'Sleep well?' he asked, noticing how her tousled hair spread over her shoulders like a silken cloud.

She grabbed her mane with both hands and pulled it behind her shoulders. 'Yeah. I must have really been out of it last night. I don't remember going to bed.'

'You didn't, actually. I put you there.' He placed a glass of orange juice in front of her, knowing it was her favourite. In the next breath he waited for her to draw the obvious conclusion.

'Then you...' Her voice faded.

'I thought you'd sleep better if you weren't so...confined.'

Her face turned pink and she sipped her juice. 'I'll appreciate your actions just as soon as I get over my embarrassment.'

'Don't be embarrassed. You're a beautiful lady.'

'Flatterer.'

'It's true,' he insisted, aware that she doubted his sincerity. 'You are.'

Her skin colour turned a darker shade. 'Thanks.'

'In fact,' he said boldly, 'I'd love to have you spend the night every night.'

Her startled gaze met his unwavering one. 'You're serious, aren't you?'

'Yes. Of course, I'm talking a legal arrangement. The "till death do us part" type.'

'Why me?'

'Because we're friends.'

She ran her finger over the lip of the glass. 'I have lots of friends. Why should I marry you over some-one else?'

He thought quickly. 'Because we're compatible.'

'This isn't a blood transfusion.'

'We mesh,' he insisted. 'We function on the same wavelength, care about the same things, have the same interests.'

Katie held the glass to her mouth. 'I know several people—men—who fit your criteria. I certainly don't want to marry any of them.'

'All right, then. I need you. Daniel needs you.'

'Yes, but—'

He pulled her to her feet and into his arms. 'You're talking entirely too much.'

Before she could utter a word he kissed her slowly and thoroughly.

A fire began to burn inside his belly. Her essence tantalised every sense he possessed until he thought he would burst into flames.

The chemical reaction generated was far greater than he'd expected or imagined. While he hadn't considered sleeping with her to be a chore, he certainly hadn't anticipated fireworks.

And, oh, what marvellous fireworks they were!

Daniel's voice, as he sang one of his pre-school songs, reminded J.D. of the great potential for interruption—and questions. With great reluctance, he tore his mouth away from Katie's.

The glazed look in her eyes made him smile. 'Looks like we're compatible in other areas, too.'

'Why did you do that?' she asked, touching her mouth.

'You said you wanted to practise. Just trying to help.'

The doorbell chimed. 'Eat your breakfast,' he ordered kindly. 'I'll see who's here.'

Before J.D. walked two steps, Daniel's excited voice brought a feeling of dread to his heart.

'It's Grandma!'

CHAPTER EIGHT

J.D. LOOKED at Katie, his plans for the weekend dying a quick, painful death. 'She must have decided to drop in for Daniel's programme,' he said weakly.

'I think it's nice she took time to come,' Katie said, apparently recovering. 'You'd better let her in before she wonders why you're leaving her on the porch.'

By the time J.D. reached the door, Daniel had already flung it open. 'Hi, Grandma.'

Virginia Berkley crouched down and held out her arms to give her grandson a bear hug. 'Hello, Daniel. I missed you.'

J.D.'s gaze, however, didn't linger on his mother. A tall, auburn-haired woman who'd accompanied Virginia and waited near the entrance drew his stunned attention.

'Rose?' he asked, uncertain if the voluptuous girl in front of him was the same girl he knew from his younger days.

Rose smiled. 'In the flesh. I hope you don't mind my unexpected arrival, but your mother told me about your son's programme. It sounded like fun, so when she invited me to keep her company on the trip out here I accepted.'

'Your father was committed to a golf tournament,' Virginia explained, 'and couldn't find a replacement. Rose just moved back to Dallas and because it's been ages since you two saw each other I thought to myself, wouldn't it be wonderful if you young people became reacquainted? You were such good friends in high school.'

Out of the corner of his eye J.D. saw Katie standing on the threshold between the kitchen and living room. Apparently Virginia did too, because she glanced in that direction, then did a double take.

'Katie Alexander? Is that you?'

'In the flesh,' Katie quipped.

'My goodness. I never would have guessed. You certainly have changed.' For the first time ever, J.D. saw his mother at a loss for words.

Katie smiled. 'So I've been told.'

'Katie?' J.D. began, uncomfortable at being in a situation with such great potential for disaster. 'This is Rose Whitlow. We went to high school together.'

'Pleased to meet you,' Katie murmured. 'So you came for Daniel's programme. He's always delighted to have people watch him perform.'

Rose bestowed a benevolent smile on Daniel. 'Children love being the centre of attention. When I taught elementary school, my students enjoyed showing off their accomplishments.'

'I hope we're not interrupting anything,' Virginia said, her attention bouncing back and forth between J.D. and Katie. 'But you did say I could come any time.'

'No problem, Mom.' J.D. gave Katie a sidelong glance, wondering if anyone else had noticed her thoroughly kissed appearance.

'You're not interrupting, Grandma,' Daniel said. 'Katie and Daddy just got up. Daddy was fixing breakfast and lunch together.'

J.D. recognised his mother's imperceptible narrowing of her eyes. Thanks, Danny boy, he thought to himself.

He squared his shoulders and met his mother's gaze. He didn't owe her—or anyone else, for that matter—an explanation. He was an adult—what he did was his business and his alone. It was a shame that he'd been found guilty of a crime he'd *wanted* to commit, but hadn't.

'Our bags are in the car, J.D,' Virginia announced. 'Would you mind bringing them in for us?'

J.D. had no intention of leaving Katie alone with his mother, especially not since he saw a speculative gleam in her eye. 'In a minute. You've had a long drive. There's coffee in the kitchen. Help yourself.'

He grabbed Katie's elbow, ushered her to the guest room before Virginia and Rose could utter a word in protest and closed the door. 'I had no idea my mother was coming, much less that she'd bring someone with her.'

Katie's smile seemed dim and she started stripping the sheets off the bed she'd slept in. 'I know.'

'I had our weekend all planned,' he began.

'It's OK, J.D.' She paused. 'Rose is beautiful, isn't she?'

He took the opposite side and helped her smooth a fresh set over the mattress. 'I guess.'

'She is. Did you notice her freckles?'

'No, I didn't.' He was starting to feel as if his carefully crafted list was going to be more of a hindrance than a help.

'I'll bet she's a terrific athlete. Tennis, perhaps?' She raised one eyebrow.

'And basketball,' he admitted reluctantly, dredging up the fact from his memory. 'If I recall, your high school class wouldn't have called you Ms Mermaid if you didn't excel in swimming.' He referred to the moniker someone had used to describe Katie in her yearbook.

'Ancient history. From what I can see, she fills all of your qualifications perfectly.'

He tried to think of what he'd written and his mind went blank. 'For the record, we weren't as close as you think. I haven't heard from her or even *thought* of her in years.'

'It doesn't matter, J.D.,' she said softly.

To him, it most certainly did. He could already sense the wall being built between them. 'We were debate partners one semester. We never went on a date.'

'Now's the time for you to rectify the situation.'

'But I don't *want* to.'

'Your mother expects it. She's matchmaking.'

'I know, and I don't care. I'll find my own bride.'

She paused. 'Why don't you discuss this with her? In the meantime, I'm going home.'

Aware of the futility of an argument, he said, 'I'll pick you up tomorrow for Daniel's programme.'

'I can get there by myself.'

'The van has plenty of room,' he stated firmly. 'I *will* drive by to get you.'

She sighed. 'If you insist.'

'I do.'

Katie tucked the bedspread around the pillows, then thrust the wad of sheets at J.D. 'Toss those in the washer for me, would you, please?'

He grabbed the bundle, conscious of Katie's

sweet fragrance lingering on the cotton. 'You realise you're running away.'

'Your mother wants you to get reacquainted with Rose. I think it's a wise idea and so I'm encouraging you to do so. If you want to read something else into it, that's your prerogative.'

Without waiting for his reply, she headed out of the bedroom. She said her goodbyes to Virginia and Daniel, and said politely to Rose, 'It was nice to meet you.' Then Katie left.

In spite of having three extra people in the house, J.D. had never felt so alone.

The basement of the Tiny Tots Pre-school building was filling rapidly with family members. J.D. hung by the stairwell door, waiting and watching for Katie to arrive. He should have suspected she'd fabricate some excuse to avoid carpooling to the programme. He also should have suspected that she'd leave her message with his mother, thereby avoiding a lengthy explanation.

'If we don't sit down soon,' Virginia said, 'we won't find a place.'

The tread of footsteps and the chatter of voices heralded another arrival, but Katie wasn't in the group. J.D. cast another glance at the door, willing her to appear.

Rose touched his arm, looking elegant in her white designer suit. Although the fabric was beautiful, in J.D.'s opinion the colour wasn't practical for spending an afternoon around children.

'Why don't your mother and I find some seats? When Katie gets here, you can join us,' she said.

Virginia interrupted. 'The programme will start in five minutes. Perhaps she isn't coming.'

'She'll be here,' J.D. said with conviction. 'Katie won't disappoint Daniel.'

'Of course not,' Rose said. She pointed to a row of chairs near the middle. 'Virginia, why don't we claim those before someone else does?'

J.D. gave Rose a grateful smile before she moved away with his mother. He glanced at his watch, hardly able to believe that Katie would be late. Punctuality was her middle name.

Mrs Casey walked onto the makeshift stage at the front of the open room. 'If you'll take your places, we'll begin in a few minutes.'

Impulsively, J.D. darted up the steps to search for a phone. At the top he ran into Katie.

'Where've you been?' he asked, grabbing her arm to escort her down the stairs. 'The show's about to start.'

'I know,' she said breathlessly. 'I didn't realise I was driving on fumes so I detoured to a filling station. Then, when I took the nozzle out of the pump, I was in a hurry and managed to slosh gasoline on me. So I ran home to change my dress.'

J.D. eyed her black and white ensemble with appreciation. 'You look nice.'

'Thank you.'

'We saved you a seat,' he said as they reached the bottom.

She stopped short. 'Maybe I should stay in the back. I mean, your mother and Rose are here... I don't want to be in the way.'

'You won't be.' He guided her forward, careful to maintain a gentle hold on her arm. Letting her sit off in the corner by herself like some orphan, that was out of the question.

True to her word, Rose had found four seats together. She sat in a folding chair next to Virginia. J.D. offered the next one to Katie and took the aisle spot for himself.

J.D. watched Daniel file in with the other members of his class, looking like a miniature version of himself in black trousers, a light blue shirt and a clip-on blue and grey tie.

J.D. leaned closer to Katie. 'He looks great.'

'The nicest of the bunch.' In J.D.'s opinion, her smile resembled that of a proud parent.

The antics to accompany the musical numbers brought many smiles and chuckles to the crowd. Daniel's part in the 'Five Little Turkeys' number earned him applause at the way he recited his part of the poem.

'His gobble sounds so real,' he murmured to Katie.

Her eyes glowed with pride. 'We practised every afternoon.'

'Look at him grin. We may have a movie star in the making.' J.D. gave Daniel a thumbs-up sign and the smile on his little face grew even wider.

After the programme ended, Mrs Casey invited everyone to stay for refreshments and to tour the classrooms upstairs.

Daniel squeezed through the throng to reach Katie's side. 'I didn't make any mistakes,' he exclaimed.

Katie hugged him. 'You were absolutely perfect. I'm so proud of you.'

'Did you see me, Daddy? Did you see me,

Grandma?' He tugged on his father's hand. 'I'm ready for some punch, Daddy.'

For the next hour J.D. looked at walls and walls of artwork as Daniel pointed out the pieces that he'd drawn or coloured. At one point J.D. lost Katie in the crowd, but found her about fifteen minutes later.

'Hey,' he said, 'where did you wander off to?'

'Just around.' The shortness of her reply and the stiff set to her shoulders warned him of a problem.

'What's wrong? Is your knee bothering you?'

She blinked. 'My knee? Oh, yeah. It's my knee.'

'Why don't you sit down for a while?'

'I'm all right. Look.' She motioned toward the opposite side of the room. 'Martha and Henrietta are here.'

Daniel was delighted to hear of the presence of his two surrogate grandmothers. 'I bet I have the mostest people here,' he boasted.

'And you need to thank each of them for coming,' Katie told him.

While Daniel dutifully ran off to obey, another mother who stood nearby commented, 'Your son is so polite. You both must be pleased.'

'We are,' J.D. said smoothly, aware that his mother had overheard from her spot only a few feet away. The woman moved towards the next display and Katie confronted him in a low voice.

'Why did you let her think he was our son?'

'I didn't feel like giving any explanations,' he answered. 'Does it bother you if people think he's yours?'

'No, but—'

Mrs Casey joined them at that moment. 'How

good of you to come,' she said, smiling at both Virginia and Rose. 'What a nice surprise for Daniel.'

'Yes, it was,' J.D. said. But, as surprises went, he reserved judgement on classifying it as 'nice'.

'I'll be sending the artwork home next week, so be prepared,' Mrs Casey warned with a smile, before greeting another family.

Daniel returned, munching on another cookie.

'I think that's enough, young man,' J.D. said. 'You'll ruin your supper.'

'That's right, Daniel,' Virginia said. 'Since you're dressed so handsomely, I made a five-thirty reservation for us at the country club.'

J.D. frowned. His mother was up to something. 'Katie and I had planned on grilling hamburgers at home, Mom. I told you that this morning.'

Virginia waved her manicured hand. 'This is a special occasion and I intend to treat it like one.'

Suddenly, dismay flitted across her features. 'Oh, dear. I only requested a table for four. I don't know what I was thinking. You don't mind, do you, Katie?'

J.D. was willing to bet his solid silver tie tac that his mother hadn't erred by accident. 'That's easily rectified. I'll call and correct our reservation. If they can't accommodate us, we'll go someplace else.'

'Please don't change it on my account,' Katie answered politely. 'Enjoy your meal.' She ruffled Daniel's hair. 'See you tomorrow, sport.'

'Rose and I are staying for a few days,' Virginia interjected. 'We'll look after Daniel. I'm sure you'll appreciate having some time for yourself.'

'Mother,' J.D. ground out.

Katie touched his forearm. 'It's OK. Please don't

make an issue.' She glanced down at the little boy.
'I'll see you later, Daniel.'

Katie disappeared in the crowd before J.D. could
object. 'Let's go,' he said tersely, telegraphing his
displeasure to his parent. Taking Daniel's hand, he
strode out of the building at a fast clip.

As testimony to Virginia's ability to carry on a
conversation under the most difficult of circum-
stances, she chatted with Rose and Daniel during the
drive home as if she didn't have a care in the world.
J.D., however, was too incensed to say anything.

After he'd parked his vehicle in the garage, he
remained outside hoping for the nip in the air to cool
his temper. Going into the back yard, he began
clearing the dead vegetation out of their small gar-
den spot—the spot Katie had hounded him to create
so Daniel could watch his seeds grow.

He'd pulled all of the tomato plants when he noticed his mother standing on the patio.

'You'll ruin your clothes.'

'They'll wash.'

'You're angry with me—'

'Now, there's an understatement.' He uprooted a
dried up cucumber vine and tossed it on the growing
pile.

'I just think you and Rose deserve a chance to
get to know each other.'

He stopped to stare at her. 'Speaking of Rose, you
shouldn't have brought her without giving me some
advance notice.'

'You'd have said no.'

'Damned right, I would have said no. I can take
care of my own love life. I don't need your interference.'

Virginia sighed. 'I wanted to help.'

'You aren't. You were rude to Katie and, considering everything she's done for Daniel and me, your actions were inexcusable.'

'I admit it and I'm sorry.' She paused. 'Do you love her?'

He hadn't thought about it before. He respected Katie, appreciated her, enjoyed her company and was physically attracted to her. Was that love?

He'd loved Ellen with his whole heart and soul. His devotion had blossomed instantly and without question. Looking back, it was as if Fate had issued a decree: the intensity of their relationship would compensate for its short duration.

His feelings for Katie, however, were very different. They had developed over time from the seeds of friendship and had only recently started to blossom into the romance he'd thought he'd never experience again.

'Yes, I love her,' he said, admitting it aloud for the first time. 'So much so that I can't imagine living my life without her.'

'She's a lot like Ellen.'

'How do you know? You never met her.' He stopped, suddenly suspicious. 'Or did you?'

Virginia avoided his gaze. 'I met her. Briefly.'

'When?' he demanded.

She hesitated.

'When, Mother?' He used a cold tone.

She heaved a dainty sigh. 'It was right after you told me about her. I had come to Kansas City for Winnifred's daughter's wedding. I called on Ellen right before the ceremony.'

He strode forward, unwilling to miss a single word of her story. 'What did you tell her?'

'I didn't discourage her, if that's what you're thinking,' she said tartly. 'We talked about general things, like living in Kansas City, her family, her job. Naturally, we discussed you, too. I invited her to Dallas, and then I left.'

J.D. rubbed the back of his neck. His mother hadn't needed to verbally dissuade Ellen. Virginia's mere arrival in a gown worthy of a society wedding—costing more than six months' worth of Ellen's rent—with Virginia's favourite diamonds dripping from her fingers, would have intimidated her beyond belief.

Ellen had always been self-conscious of growing up courtesy of the state system. Discussing her family—admitting that she didn't have one—wouldn't have instilled confidence at the idea of rubbing elbows with blue-bloods, either.

No wonder she'd written her 'Dear John' letter and vanished.

'If it's any consolation, I thought she was a lovely young woman. Unfortunately, hindsight is always perfect.' She sounded weary. 'My impatience to meet her played a role in her disappearance. You and Daniel have paid the price and for that I'm deeply sorry. I simply don't want you to go through the experience again.'

'Katie won't run out on me. She isn't like that.'

She lifted one penciled-in eyebrow. 'How can you be sure?'

'Because I know Katie.'

'Time will tell. In any case, what harm would it do to spend time with Rose?'

'Mother,' he warned.

'I'm serious,' she insisted. 'Consider the situation from this angle. Spending time with Rose will either reaffirm your feelings for Katie or point out your unsuitability before you both make a mistake. You have Daniel to consider.'

'I don't need time with Rose to know what or whom I want.'

She sighed. 'You are old enough to make your own decisions, I suppose.'

'Yes, Mom. I am.'

'Rose would make you a wonderful wife.'

'She'll make *some man* a wonderful wife,' he corrected, 'but I'm not that man.'

Virginia seemed resigned. 'I'll call Katie and apologise.'

'Good idea.' He returned to his former spot, bent down and uprooted another plant.

She started towards the door, then stopped. 'Aren't you coming in?'

'I may as well finish the job I started.' More importantly, he wanted to give his mother the time and the privacy to call Katie.

'What about Rose?'

'She's your guest, not mine.' At his mother's crestfallen expression, he relented. 'After I'm done, I'll play the attentive host. I promise.'

Virginia went through the sliding glass patio door and J.D. continued his efforts. Fifteen minutes later he followed.

His mother met him at the door. 'I've tried calling her, but she doesn't answer. It's nearly five o'clock. What should I do?'

'Keep trying while I shower,' he said.

But as the evening wore on their efforts to reach Katie failed. J.D. tried to carry on a polite conversation with Rose after their meal at the country club, but his thoughts continually strayed.

Where was Katie?

The hours seemed to drag in spite of the congenial conversation. Finally, at ten p.m., Rose called it a day. 'I'd forgotten how energetic small children are,' she said ruefully. 'Goodnight.'

Virginia excused herself, too, and J.D. didn't waste a moment contemplating his next move. He grabbed the keys to his van, let himself out of the house and drove towards Katie's home.

Her car was gone, the house dark. On impulse, he passed down several of her friends' streets, but her silver Toyota wasn't anywhere to be found. To his relief, it wasn't in front of Hank's apartment either.

Conceding defeat, he backtracked to his garage and consoled himself with the prospect of seeing her at work in the morning.

J.D. strode into the ER thirty minutes earlier than usual and saw Beth Lockwood at the nurses' desk. 'Where's Katie?'

Beth, the tawny-haired, thirty-year-old nursing supervisor, cast him a baleful glance. 'It's nice to know I've been gone a month and no one noticed. Hello to you, too.'

He grinned sheepishly. 'Hi, Beth. How was your vacation?'

'Wonderful,' she reported in a dreamy voice. 'Tristan was ready to come back two weeks ago, but the kids and I loved it. No schedule to follow, no appointments to meet—it was pure heaven.'

Her whimsical tone switched to normal. 'From the looks of things around here, you can't say the same.'

'No kidding.'

'What I want to know is, what did you do to Katie?'

He glanced around. 'Where is she? I need to talk to her.'

'She's with a patient. I'm not sure it would be a good idea, anyway.'

J.D. rubbed his eyes with his thumbs. 'What a mess. Did she tell you what's happened?'

'Bits and pieces. I called her yesterday to let her know we were back in town and she came over.'

So she'd gone to ground at the Lockwoods'. If he'd been thinking clearly, he would have remembered the date and could have checked with them.

Beth lowered her voice. 'She mentioned your marriage scheme.'

'Did she also tell you that I asked her to marry me? And that she refused?'

Beth tutted. 'I'm really surprised at you, J.D. You don't have a clue as to what's going on, do you?'

'Obviously, I don't.'

Marty and Ashley came out of an exam room and Beth beckoned J.D. to follow her into the privacy of their walk-in supply closet.

She lowered her voice. 'First of all, Katie loves you.'

He stared at her incredulously.

'In fact, she has for years.'

'Years? Then why in the sam ned won't she marry me?'

'Back up for a minute. Once you started searching for a wife, what did she do?

'I'll tell you what she did,' she continued before he could answer. 'Katie went through a complete transformation and do you know why? To get your attention. After waiting in the wings for you to heal from Ellen's death, she wanted you to notice her— not as a friend, or a babysitter, but as a woman.'

Beth's hypothesis made sense. Katie was like the trusty stethoscope that he took for granted. It was always available in his pocket and had never failed him.

'And, knowing Katie, she probably tried to be everything you asked for on your ridiculous list.'

He recalled his 'athletic' requirement and remembered how she'd doggedly insisted on playing football when her knee was sore.

'Then why did she recommend Cecilia and Marilyn and...' he snapped his fingers '...what's her name?'

Beth raised one eyebrow, as if waiting for him to draw the conclusion. 'You tell me.'

He thought a moment. 'She *wanted* me to find fault with them.'

'Give the doctor a cigar,' she crowed. 'Exactly.'

'Katie told you all this?'

'Like I said, only bits and pieces. After watching her for years and hearing what she's been doing lately, I put two and two together.'

'If you're right, then why did she ask for someone who's six feet two, one-eighty, dark hair and blue eyes? She went so far as to specify a manual labourer or a law-enforcement person—definitely not someone in health care.'

'Be honest. If she'd described you even in the most general of terms, at the very least you'd have been uncomfortable. In fact, you'd have probably run in the opposite direction.'

He weighed her statement and saw the truth in it.

'Katie had no choice but to throw you off the scent. Who knows? She may have been trying to make you jealous.'

'Well, it worked,' he said, thinking of Hank and Thad, 'but your theory still doesn't explain why she won't accept my proposal.'

'Did she point-blank refuse?'

'At first, but on Saturday she seemed to give the idea serious consideration. Although that was before my mother showed up with one of her cronies' daughters,' he finished ruefully.

'Ah, the old city mouse and country mouse story.'

'I suppose.'

'Katie probably feels as if she can't compete. I hate to say this, but she's like Ellen in that respect.'

He ran his hands through his hair. 'The point is, she doesn't *have* to compete. I don't *want* anyone else.'

'Then hang in there. She'll come around.'

'Yes, but what if someone else sweeps her off her feet in the meantime?'

'She won't fall for anyone else if you give her what she wants.'

'Which is?'

'You'll have to figure that one out for yourself. She didn't give me the details of her list.'

He reviewed every qualifying trait Katie had named and came up blank. A comment she'd once made teased his subconscious and he struggled to pin down the elusive memory. It hovered on the fringes of his mind, but refused to come forward.

'She'd mentioned something,' he said slowly, 'but I can't think of what it was.'

'It'll come to you. And when it does, don't waste any time.'

'I won't.' It would be hard to concentrate on Katie with his mother and Rose in the house, but he would—even if he had to slip away under false pretences.

From outside the walk-in storage closet, J.D. heard a feminine voice mention his name. He stepped to the doorway and saw Ashley in conversation with another nurse.

'There you are,' Ashley exclaimed. 'Katie's been looking for you.'

'She has?' he asked, trying not to let his elation show.

Ashley pointed down the hall. 'She went that way.'

Bolstered by Beth's encouraging nod, J.D. went to find her. Just as he passed by the last room, the door opened and Katie came barrelling out.

He gave her an encouraging smile. 'Ashley said you wanted to see me.'

She closed the door behind her. 'Marty needs a consult and you have a visitor.'

A strange sense of history repeating itself came over him. 'A visitor? It's not my mother, is it?'

Katie thrust a clipboard at him. 'You're close. It's Rose.'

CHAPTER NINE

'ROSE?' J.D. asked, incredulous. 'What is *she* doing here?'

'I don't know. I didn't ask. You'll find her in the lounge.'

He would have understood anger on Katie's part, or supreme hurt or coolness, but her stoicism caught him off guard. It was as if she were a polite but uncaring stranger who had passed him on the street.

'About yesterday,' he began. 'I want to apologise for my mother's behaviour. She had no right to exclude you and I told her so.'

She avoided his gaze. 'Hey, don't worry about it. Like she said, you needed time with Rose.'

'Like my mother said?' he uttered. 'When did she say this?'

'At Daniel's programme. We were in his classroom when she cornered me.'

J.D. couldn't remember seeing his mother alone with Katie, although at one point the women had disappeared. Obviously Virginia, not the crowd, had engineered their separation.

His eyes narrowed in suspicion. 'What else did she say?'

'Nothing that I didn't already know, or at least suspect.'

'Which was?'

This time Katie looked directly at him. 'You have

to kiss a lot of frogs to find a prince. Or, in your case, a princess.'

He was starting to feel aggravated at all the women in his life. Every one seemed to think she knew his mind better than he did.

'You're not going to find your princess if this particular frog is always underfoot,' she continued.

J.D. saw red. 'My mother said *that*?'

'I'm not quoting her, but the message was the same. Now, don't get upset. Admittedly, I was at first, but I've thought about the situation and she's right. In fact, I mentioned it to you several weeks ago.'

'This is crazy.'

'No, it's not. Daniel has to accept his future mother and he won't if I'm the one he depends on. So I've come to a decision. It's time to cut the umbilical cord.'

'You can't do that.'

'I have to,' she said gently. 'It's the only way we'll move forward with our lives. We've both become too comfortable with our arrangement and I refuse to drift into a marriage because we happen to get along with each other.'

He opened his mouth to speak, but she tapped the clipboard with her knuckles. 'Marty is chomping at the bit for you to see this patient. He's waiting for the blood gas results and you have her chart. And when you're finished with this consult, don't forget Rose.'

Aggravated by his inability to deal with the problem at hand, he ground his teeth together. 'Realise this. Our discussion isn't over. It's only postponed. So be prepared.'

Consoled by his pledge, he scanned the patient complaint recorded in Katie's neat handwriting. Wendy Xavier, twenty-six.

'What's the story?' he asked.

'She has signs of a classic panic attack. Tightness in her chest, difficulty in breathing.'

'Chest X-Ray?'

Marty met them outside Wendy's room, carrying a page hot off the lab printer. 'Normal. Her ABG is borderline normal, too. I considered a blood clot until the results came out OK.'

'We can't totally rule out a pulmonary embolism from these tests,' J.D. said. 'Is she on any medication?'

'OTC pain relievers and the Pill,' Katie supplied.

Mention of the oral contraceptive waved a red flag in J.D.'s mind. 'That gives her a predisposing factor for your diagnosis,' he mentioned to Marty. 'I'll check her and then we'll decide where to go next.'

Katie accompanied him into the cubicle where he introduced himself. 'I know you've told your symptoms to the nurse and our physician's assistant, but I want you to go over them once more with me.'

Wendy was a pretty young woman with rosy red cheeks. 'Can't breathe,' she mumbled. 'I went to work and then from out of the blue, it felt like someone put a tight band around my chest. Couldn't catch my breath.'

'What do you do for a living?' he asked, placing his stethoscope over her hospital gown to listen.

'Secretary.'

'Ever taken any drugs?' he asked.

She hesitated, as if debating whether honesty was the best policy or not.

'It will remain strictly confidential,' he encouraged.

'Marijuana. About a year ago.'

J.D. continued his assessment, but once he'd finished he was as stumped as Marty had been. He'd hoped to find some clue, some small overlooked piece of information which would steer him toward an explanation.

He found none.

Leaning against the sink, he crossed his arms. 'Wendy, you might have what we call a pulmonary embolus, which is a fancy term for a blood clot on your lung.'

She gasped. 'A blood clot? Me?'

'Before we can be certain, we'll have to run a lot more tests.' He thought of lung scans and pulmonary arteriography.

Her eyes widened with fright.

He decided to play a hunch. 'On the other hand,' he said, his voice stern, 'those procedures are extremely expensive. I need to know the truth, Wendy. Are you doing drugs?'

She studied her fingernails for a few seconds before she nodded.

He pressed on. 'Cocaine?'

Once again she nodded. 'When I got up this morning and again after I got to work.'

'And then you started to feel bad?'

'Yeah.'

'Thanks for coming clean,' he said lightly. 'I can now tell you this. Your symptoms are due to the cocaine and will wear off as the day goes on.'

Relief flooded across her face.

He decided to take advantage of the situation to

inject the proverbial fear of God into her. 'People don't understand that cocaine does more than give them a mental buzz. It beats the heck out of the blood vessels. The drug tells the arteries to constrict or squeeze, which in turn causes strokes, heart attacks, muscle necrosis, kidney failure and lung problems.

'It also inflames the linings of the blood vessels to the extent of creating blood clots and aneurysms. I don't need to tell you those are highly fatal conditions.'

Her face blanched when he mentioned aneurysm. Perhaps she would think twice about continuing on her path of destruction. He hoped so.

'Two things, though,' he added. 'One. Never, *ever* lie to your doctor again.'

'I won't,' she promised.

'And, two, kick your habit. There are some wonderful treatment centres in Kansas City. Check into one.'

'But I just got this job,' she wailed. 'My insurance won't cover rehab and I can't afford to pay for it out of my own pocket.'

'After what I just told you, you can't afford not to,' he told her. 'Katie will give you some brochures. Take them home, study them and think long and hard about what you put in your body. OK?'

She gave him a tremulous smile. 'OK.'

Outside the exam room Katie asked, 'Do you think you did any good?'

He raised one shoulder in a shrug. 'If nothing else, she can't claim ignorance.'

After a brief discussion with Marty, and conscious

of how long Rose had been waiting, J.D. hurried to the lounge.

'Sorry to keep you waiting,' he said as soon as he saw her standing near the bulletin board papered with notices of upcoming staff meetings, sign-up sheets for the annual ER Thanksgiving dinner and 'For Sale' ads.

Rose turned to greet him. She looked perfect, not a hair out of place. Her trousers and shirt were Nieman Marcus quality and probably cost a small fortune.

He thought of Katie's question about spending habits. Knowing the wealth in Rose's family and the upbringing it afforded her, pinching pennies wasn't one of the life skills she had learned.

'I understand. I shouldn't have dropped in unexpectedly so I was prepared to wait.'

'Coffee?' he asked, holding up the pot.

She declined and he filled his Viagra mug. After a cautious sip he realised that Katie had made it and so he drank deeply. 'What brings you here?' he finally asked.

'I wanted to thank you for your hospitality. Virginia and I are leaving after lunch.'

'You are?' He tried not to sound relieved. Entertaining Rose while trying to mend his fences with Katie had seemed like an impossible juggling feat.

'I always liked you, J.D.,' she began. 'Your mother had told me all about you and Daniel so I thought now was a good time to see if we could click. If I'd known there was someone else...'

'I'm sorry,' he said sincerely.

She smiled. 'Me, too. But it's for the best. Katie's a great lady.'

'I think so.'

'Daniel talks about her all the time. He really loves her. No one else could replace her in his affections.'

Rose cleared her throat before she continued. 'In any case, I'll be expecting a wedding invitation.'

He grinned. 'I'll put your name on my list.'

She crossed the room, raised herself on tiptoe and kissed him on the cheek. 'Goodbye, J.D. Give me a call if for some reason things don't work out.'

He refused to think negatively. 'They will.'

What seemed a split second later, Ashley poked her head inside. 'Dr Casey wants to see you in his office right away.'

Uneasy at the way her eyes followed the path of his hand on Rose's back, J.D. let his arm drop. 'Thanks,' he said. 'I'll be right there.'

'Uh-oh,' Rose teased. 'What have you done now?'

'Nothing. At least not in the last day or two,' he amended.

'Better not keep the head honcho waiting,' she said. 'I suspect he won't be as patient as I was. And let me know about the wedding date.'

'Fair enough.' Conscious of Ashley watching their exchange with interest, he glowered at the nurse. She blushed, then quickly fled while J.D. headed down the opposite corridor.

Robert Casey's office was adjacent to Allan's and J.D. reached it in minutes.

'What's going on?' he asked the medical director as he took a seat. Every time J.D. crossed the threshold the sense of isolation always amazed him. A totally different world existed only a short distance away.

'Trouble,' Robert announced without preamble. 'Word of the lawn incident has reached our board of directors' ears. Several of them are calling for a censure because of your failure to obey hospital policy.'

J.D. was totally unprepared for this. 'What?'

'Some are up in arms over the fact that you left the ER unattended, which is why the policy was written in the first place.'

J.D. muttered an expletive.

'They're concerned about what our liability would have been if an ambulance had delivered a trauma to Mercer's door and we hadn't had a physician available.'

'That's a bunch of hogwash. It wouldn't have been any different if Marty and I had been tied up with another patient in another room.'

'Regardless, they're screaming for an inquiry.'

'That policy is ridiculous and you know it,' J.D. stated.

'I agree, but it's still on the books. We have to comply with what's outlined, to the letter.'

'So I should have let Mr Pollard bleed to death on the lawn while the crowd stood by?' J.D. was astonished. 'What sort of confidence in our facility would that have instilled in the public? Did the board consider our liability if we'd ignored the man?'

'I'm on your side, J.D.,' Robert said, 'But the board is right. We have to follow our policies or we open ourselves up for lawsuits.'

'In other words, we should walk by an injured person because our policy says we can't touch them before an ambulance crew does?' J.D. shook his head. 'I don't know about you, but that isn't how I practise medicine.'

Robert tapped his pen against his desk blotter. 'The board has called a special meeting on Friday to discuss these issues. We have four days to prepare.'

'The best defence I can think of is to ask them one question. Would they have wanted me to wait for an ambulance if the person on the lawn had been a member of *their* family?'

'It's difficult to write a policy to cover every situation because there are exceptions to every rule. Off the record, however, I'd have made the same decision.'

Robert's reassurance made J.D. feel slightly better.

'In the meantime, it might be a good idea to revamp the procedure and present it to them at this meeting.'

'I'll work on it,' J.D. said.

'You should also be prepared for the worst. I've heard mutterings from certain board members who believe that if we have time to search out patients to treat then we aren't busy enough to justify creating a centre dedicated to minor injuries.'

J.D. stared at the older man. 'I didn't solicit this man's business. He came to us. Admittedly, he didn't make it all the way, but he was trying. It isn't as if we treat patients on the front lawn on a daily basis. This was an isolated incident—it's never happened before in the four years I've been here and it probably won't happen again for another four.'

'Those are the issues we'll point out. I only mentioned it because the best defence is a good offence.'

J.D. set his jaw. Of all days, he didn't need the extra aggravation this news gave him.

'In any case, be available at two o'clock on Friday,' Robert ordered.

Summarily dismissed, J.D. retraced his steps to the ER.

'Why the glum face?' Beth asked him.

He explained, finishing with 'I have four days to prepare a case eloquent enough to salvage both my job and my minor emergency centre proposal.'

'Tristan and I will help in any way we can,' she promised.

'Thanks.'

He glanced about him. 'Is Katie around?'

Beth winced. 'She left.'

'Left?'

'She received a phone call and then asked for emergency vacation leave. Apparently someone on the ambulance crew had a death in the family and will be gone all week. As they're critically understaffed, the chief called her and asked if she could possibly fill in until the guy returned.'

'And you let her go?'

Beth appeared affronted. 'What could I say? Now that I'm back we're fully staffed. I didn't have any reason to deny her request.'

'Dammit, Beth. How in the world am I supposed to talk to her if she isn't even here?'

'You're a resourceful person. You'll think of

something. Don't forget, she's on the ambulance crew. She'll be in and out of here all day long.'

To J.D.'s consternation, Beth's prediction didn't come to pass. The ER bustled with cases, but none came by ambulance. He also didn't have any luck in reaching her that evening and bemoaned the situation to Beth on Tuesday.

'She had a date with someone named Frankie,' Beth said. 'She didn't seem impressed when I talked to her, but if I were you I'd send flowers.'

'Good idea.' He took advantage of a few spare minutes to order a dozen long-stemmed red roses.

After work, J.D. stopped at the library to return Daniel's books. As he passed a section featuring poets he stopped to browse through a book of quotations. In it he found an old Polish proverb about a man finding love through his eyes while a woman found love through her ears.

He thought back to that fateful Saturday, wondering what he could have said or done differently. He'd suggested entering into a legal arrangement for several reasons. One, they were friends.

Didn't the most stable marriages possess a bond of friendship?

Two, he'd spoken of their compatibility. He'd learned to read her moods and anticipate her thoughts, as she had his. Not only did they share similar interests, but he'd sampled a taste of the fulfilment they would find in a physical relationship.

Third, he'd mentioned need, both his and Daniel's. She knew how much they relied upon her. She sewed Daniel's costumes, taught him his songs, helped him with his alphabet and numbers and took him shopping.

J.D. needed her to bring normalcy to their lives, to add the soft touches necessary to smooth out his rough edges. She had a gift for caring and had utilised her gift during her entire life, first with her mother, then her brother, and now him and his son.

Need isn't the same as love.

The thought came from nowhere, as if an otherworldly being had dropped it inside his skull. The subsequent revelation was like the mystery door on a game show, opening to reveal the prize inside.

Katie Alexander didn't want people to *need* her; someone had needed her for something or other her entire life.

Katie Alexander wanted someone to *want* her, not for what she could do but for who she was. She wanted a grand passion. The comment he'd been racking his brain to remember reverberated through his mind like a pistol shot.

No wonder she hadn't jumped at his platonic marriage offer, even if, as Beth had said, Katie had loved him for years. He'd been appealing to her logic when she was hungry for an ardent romance—for someone to pay her special attention.

His tactics had been all wrong. He should have been wining and dining her at private restaurants—the kind with candles and roses on the table. He should have arranged to take her to concerts and plays in Kansas City.

He should have told her that he loved her.

Anxious to right his wrongs, he tried calling her on Wednesday, but she wasn't available. Frustrated by his run of seemingly bad luck, he stewed over matters for the next several hours until his plan came together.

At four that afternoon he overheard a squad reporting the condition of a patient in transit. He recognised the female voice reciting the details and his heart raced with excitement. Her days of ignoring him were coming to a close.

'We have a thirteen-year-old patient who was hit in the left chest at football practice. He's complaining of rib tenderness, chest pain and difficulty in breathing. We have him on O2. Saturation is OK. BP is 140 over 70. ETA is five minutes.'

Beth spoke into the mike. 'Ten-four, squad ten.'

'Notify Radiology,' J.D. ordered. 'We'll need to know if he's cracked any ribs.'

The ambulance arrived with its usual fanfare. J.D. met them at the door, allowing himself only a brief glimpse of Katie in her trim blue uniform before focusing on the youth.

'This is Trent Bradley,' Katie reported as they pushed the teenager into a trauma room and transferred him to a hospital gurney. 'He's a fullback.'

'How're you doing, Trent?' J.D. asked.

'Not so good,' the boy answered.

J.D. quickly examined him, noticing the bruising and swelling on the left side of his ribcage. 'We're going to get a few X-Rays,' he told the coach, who was hovering in the background.

'I've called his parents,' the man said.

'Good.'

'Mom's gonna kill me,' Trent moaned.

'Why's that?' J.D. asked.

'She didn't want me playing football this year. Said it was too rough.'

'Mothers worry over things like that. So do fathers,' he added, thinking of how he'd react if Daniel wanted to play football someday.

J.D. motioned to the X-Ray tech to take over. Noticing Katie and her partner, Doug, were preparing to leave, he issued an order from across the room.

'Don't leave yet, guys.'

'We'll wait outside,' Doug said.

J.D. met them several minutes later. He grabbed Katie's elbow and steered her towards the walk-in storage closet, speaking over his shoulder to a startled Doug. 'I'll bring her back in a little while. Help yourself to a cup of coffee and some of Ashley's cookies.'

'What are you doing?' Katie scolded.

'Trying to find out why you've ignored my messages the last few days.'

She blushed. 'I couldn't call you here, and I refused to catch you at home. Not with your mother and Rose in the house. I'm not a glutton for punishment.'

'They left on Monday. Rose came to say goodbye.'

'Really?' A wrinkle appeared on her forehead. 'They didn't stay long.'

He gave an unconcerned shrug. 'She and I both knew from the beginning that a relationship wouldn't work.'

Katie frowned. 'You're kidding. I thought Rose was perfect for you.'

'I'd have to work two jobs to keep her in the style she's accustomed to.' He thought he saw a glimmer of relief on her face, but he wasn't absolutely certain.

'Thanks for the flowers,' she said. 'They're beautiful.'

To think he'd been worried over how to conduct a romance. There was nothing to it. He grinned. 'Glad you liked them.'

'I know you're trying to apologise for your mother by sending roses, but it wasn't necessary.'

He was dumbstruck. 'Apologise?'

'Sure. Why else would you have sent them? It's not my birthday.'

His grin froze. Flowers, especially roses, had seemed like a foolproof romantic gesture. Apparently he'd been wrong.

'I was hoping you'd come over on Friday,' he said gruffly, setting his plan in motion.

'If you're going to spend the night telling me how compatible we are—'

He held up his hand. 'I won't. I promise. You don't want to drift into marriage and I wholeheartedly agree.'

She blinked. 'You do?'

'Absolutely. I want to sail full steam ahead into wedded bliss, not float into it because the tide has carried me there.' At her hesitation, he tried to sweeten the deal. 'Someone I know wants to meet you.'

'No kidding? Who is he?'

'It's a surprise. I don't want you to form any preconceived ideas.'

'In other words, be prepared for disappointment.'

'Hey.' He pretended affront. 'Would I steer you wrong?'

'After setting me up with Milt and Frankie, you

really don't want me to answer your question, do you? Answer this, though. He's a real dog, isn't he?'

'Now, now. Beauty is in the eye of the beholder. Are you coming?'

Katie chewed on her bottom lip. 'I suppose. It will have to be late, though. After eight.'

'Works for me,' he said cheerfully, mentally outlining the details. He'd talk Beth into keeping Daniel overnight so he could set a romantic stage worthy of the movies and confess his feelings without interruption. He also intended to give her a dose of the grand passion she wanted. By the time morning dawned, Katie wouldn't dare accuse him of proposing to her for convenience's sake.

The radio on her belt squawked with the dispatcher's voice. 'Squad ten. Are you available?'

Katie answered. 'Ten-four.'

J.D. listened as the dispatcher reported an elderly woman who'd fallen in her home and needed assistance.

'Gotta go,' she told him.

Pleased by the positive bent to the situation, his mood brightened. And when Daniel wanted to see Katie on Thursday, J.D. thought it an excellent idea.

He wasn't above playing on her soft spot where Daniel was concerned—he'd use any weapon he possibly could.

Delaying Daniel's bedtime by half an hour, J.D. hurried home after his shift ended and found Martha had Daniel ready for their outing. They drove to the station, went inside and asked for Katie.

'I don't think she's left yet,' Doug told them. 'Check the rec room.'

Following his directions, J.D. and Daniel soon

found the area where the EMTs and paramedics could relax by playing billiards, watching television or simply doing nothing.

Katie's face lit up as soon as she saw them. 'Hi, guys. What are you doing here?'

Daniel handed her the picture he'd created. 'We bringed you a present.'

Katie took the drawing and smiled. 'This is wonderful, Daniel. Thank you so much.'

Daniel stared at the big-screen television. 'Is this where you work?' he asked, incredulous.

She grinned. 'Sometimes.'

He screwed his face into a frown. 'Then you don't work with my daddy any more?'

'Yes, I do. I'm just working here this week.'

'Ah.' Clearly intrigued by the billiard table, he wandered in that direction to study the pool cues.

'It was nice of you to come,' she said.

'Daniel missed you,' J.D. said simply.

She responded with a nod.

'I have, too,' he added.

This time, her smile seemed forced. 'I've been doing a lot of thinking the past few days.'

'Katie?' Daniel interrupted. 'Can I play with the balls?'

'Just keep them on the table,' she said. Then she hesitated, as if she'd lost her train of thought.

'You've been thinking,' J.D. prompted.

Her act of drawing a deep breath and squaring her shoulders seemed ominous. 'About Friday evening…' she began.

He sensed bad news. 'What about it?'

'I'm not coming.'

'Why not?'

'I don't want to meet whoever it is that wants to meet me.'

'You don't?' Intent on her answer, he ignored the sound of Daniel crashing the balls into each other.

'There's someone else…' She paused. 'I should have told you a long time ago…'

'Hey, Katie. Are you ready to go?'

The familiar voice sent a chill down J.D.'s spine. He knew without looking who had entered the room. Hank.

His heart felt heavy. 'I see.'

'No,' she corrected. 'I don't think you do. Hank came because I needed help with my car.'

The fact that she hadn't sought out *him* drove home the truth of her statement.

'I see.' J.D. called to Daniel. 'Let's go, son. It's late.'

'I'll stop by soon,' she told Daniel as he took J.D.'s hand. The little boy nodded, his expression eager.

'Come, Daniel,' J.D. ordered, anxious to leave. He didn't expect Katie to follow through with her promise. He would simply have to figure out a way to break the news gently to Daniel.

The woman his son looked upon as his mother wouldn't be coming back any more.

CHAPTER TEN

'I CAN'T believe what you've told me is true,' Beth said the next day, her eyes filled with shock. 'It's totally inconceivable.'

'If you had seen what I had seen, you wouldn't think so,' J.D. said in a short tone.

'But her actions don't make sense.'

'Maybe not, but she said she had found someone else and she should have told me about him sooner.'

'I refuse to believe it.' She shook her head as if dazed. 'I don't understand how this happened.'

'It's simple. She went looking for a grand passion and someone else gave it to her.'

'Yes, but how could she?'

He'd asked himself the same question throughout the night as the rain had pattered on the roof. He'd risen this morning, his mood as cold and bleak as the November sky.

Even if she wouldn't consider him as marriage material, they were friends—and friends consulted each other before making life-changing decisions.

'It all started because I wanted a minor emergency centre. If I'd have been happy with the status quo, the subject of me being a bachelor would never have come up.'

The whole situation had snowballed from that point on. He'd enlisted Katie's help to find a wife, which in turn had required him to help her. He'd landed himself in this predicament.

'Do you know what's really sad?' he asked. 'Not only have I lost Katie, but I'm not going to get approval for the MEC.'

'You don't know that.'

He raised one eyebrow. 'Wanna bet? The board is going to crucify me this afternoon for not following policy. I'll have as much chance of receiving the funds for a new programme as I would to be selected for the next space shuttle flight.'

'Tristan and Michael and a lot of the other physicians will support you completely. You can't give up your dream.'

J.D. rubbed his gritty eyes before taking a deep swallow of his coffee. 'No, I can't, but, to be honest, I'm not sure I have the heart for it any more.'

'You're not a quitter, J.D.,' Beth said firmly. 'It isn't part of your character.'

He supposed it wasn't. He hadn't given up his search for Ellen, and he hadn't taken the easy road by letting someone else raise his son. The board's decision might be a set-back, but he wouldn't abandon his goal.

Now, more than ever, he couldn't roll over like a trained puppy. Just as concentrating on Daniel had helped him retain his sanity after Ellen's death, the minor emergency centre would serve as his lifeline until he relegated Katie to his past.

'As for Katie,' Beth said, her voice filled with conviction, 'there's a logical explanation.'

J.D. raised one eyebrow. 'Another distinguished theory? I'm all ears.'

Beth glared at him. 'You don't have to be sarcastic. I said there was a logical explanation. We just don't know what it is.'

'She found the man of her dreams.'

'I suppose so,' she said thoughtfully. 'Still, I'm guessing that—'

'Please. Enough is enough.' He rose, then headed for the exit with his mug. 'I'm going to prepare for this afternoon's little gathering. If you need me, I'll be in the medical library.'

'You don't want to stick around? I'll post our little break room as off limits.'

That particular room had too many memories, both good and bad. 'I would if I didn't need a few reference books. There is one thing you could do for me, though.'

'Name it.'

'Keep the coffee pot full.'

'I'll do my best.' She saw the ER clerk approach with several forms in hand. 'You'd better skedaddle or you'll never get out of here.'

J.D. obeyed, grateful to have a physician's assistant and a nurse practitioner on duty to give him a much-needed break.

For the rest of the morning he pored over the old policy, pencilling in his suggestions for wording changes. As soon as he'd finished he'd send the document to a committee for approval, before presenting it to the medical staff as a whole.

His review was nearly complete when Beth rushed inside. 'Ah, did you bring more coffee?' he asked, peering into his empty mug.

She shook her head and he noticed the tense expression on her face. 'We're going to need you in about ten minutes. There's been a three-vehicle accident on Highway 54 leading into town.'

Disregarding neatness and order, he shoved the

pages into a folder and tucked it under his arm. He grabbed his mug and raced after her.

'How many and how bad?' he asked as he caught up.

'Two people are trapped in one car. They're using the jaws of life to extract them. A second vehicle— a school van—has half a dozen teenagers and an adult—I don't have any details. Apparently a cattle truck swerved to avoid the accident and ended up rolling in the ditch. The driver isn't hurt too badly but from the radio traffic, it's a real mess, with cows wandering all over the road.'

'Looks like we'll be busy for a while. Notify Surgery, the blood bank and everyone else you can think of.'

'We're already working on it.'

'With school kids involved, we'll be flooded with parents. We'll need extra security staff to keep things under control.'

By the time J.D. and Beth got downstairs and J.D. had slipped on his protective gear, the first ambulance had arrived.

'These are the worst of the family of four,' Katie told them as they wheeled in two people, both strapped to backboards with their heads and necks immobilised. 'The other two should be rolling in right behind us.'

J.D. quickly triaged a man in his late forties who was liberally covered in blood, and a young boy of approximately ten. From Katie's report and his own findings, the child was the more critical of the two.

He took him and let Marty deal with the father, noticing Katie and Doug had left shortly after they'd transferred the patients off their gurneys.

'What's your name?' J.D. asked, listening to the youngster's chest, aware of the dried blood all over his body.

'Randy' was the boy's whispered response. 'My stomach hurts real bad.' He clutched his abdomen and began to cry.

'We're going to take good care of you,' J.D. told him. 'In a little bit it won't hurt any more. I promise.'

Randy sniffled. 'Where's my dad?'

'He's on the other side of this curtain. Someone is taking care of him right now.'

'And my mom?'

'She's on her way. Just relax. We're going to do a few tests and see what's wrong so we can fix it. Do you hurt any place else?'

Randy closed his eyes and for a few seconds didn't answer. 'N-no. Just my stomach.'

J.D. turned to Ashley. 'I want labs and an abdominal X-ray. Call in Dr Lockwood.' It wouldn't hurt to have a paediatrician's opinion.

Almost immediately a lab tech arrived to draw Randy's blood and a radiology tech pushed her portable X-ray machine close to the bed.

It didn't take long for J.D. to have his answers. 'Perforated intestine,' he said, studying the films with Tristan.

Tristan agreed. 'Let's send him up to Surgery.'

As Randy disappeared down the hall, Marty stepped out from behind his curtain.

'What do you have?' J.D. asked.

'Open compound fracture of the right femur. Dr Scott is with him now.'

Mercer was fortunate to have an orthopaedic sur-

geon on staff, although there were instances when a
second specialist would have come in handy.
Today's accident had all the earmarks of being one
of those times.

Beth rushed towards them. 'I put the rest of the
family in Room Two. Mrs Brandenburg has a cut
on her forehead from the air bag, along with a possible broken wrist. Her other son, a six-year-old, got
away with a few bumps.'

'Any word on the occupants of the other car?'
J.D. asked.

'From what I've heard over the radio, the fire
crew has got one out. They're still working on the
other.'

J.D. casted Mrs Brandenburg's wrist after her X-
ray and spent his time reassuring her of Randy's and
her husband's stable conditions. He'd just finished
sewing up the gash on her forehead when Beth
poked her head inside the cubicle and motioned him
into the hallway.

'What's wrong?' he asked.

Her words tumbled out as she propelled him towards the desk—and the radio. 'Two ambulance
personnel were injured on the scene.'

He stopped short. 'What?'

'As near as I can tell from monitoring the trans-
missions, someone drove through the police barri-
cade. The car struck at least one of the EMTs working on the patient the fire department crew just
removed from the crushed vehicle.'

His stomach sank. 'Katie?'

A furrow appeared between Beth's eyebrows and
her eyes were dull with worry. 'I don't know. No
one's mentioned any details.'

The doors whooshed open and Hank strode in. At J.D.'s questioning glance, he explained. 'I'm here to help with crowd control.'

'Have you heard anything about the EMTs who were injured?' J.D. asked, hoping the policeman would have more up-to-date information.

'No.'

'Katie's out there,' he said, in case the officer hadn't realised. 'She might be one of them.'

'I hope not.'

J.D. frowned. 'You don't sound very concerned.'

'I'm sure she's fine.'

J.D. glared at him, ready to lambaste him for his callous attitude, but the radio squawked to life.

One of the sheriff's deputies asked if another ambulance was *en route*. Someone else volunteered the information that more EMS crews were being called in to assist.

An idea began to take shape. 'I could go,' he said, thinking aloud.

Beth was horrified. 'You can't. Look what happened when you went to the front lawn of the hospital. If you leave the grounds, I don't want to think about what they'll do to you.'

'I have to go,' he said. The thought of Katie hurt, with no one to help her but a few first-aid-trained sheriff's officers, was enough to spur him into action.

'Who's going to handle your job here while you're gone?' she pointed out.

'Call Michael.'

'I tried, but he isn't home.'

The idea of waiting helplessly grated on J.D.'s nerves.

'Call for a status report,' she urged. 'If she's in bad shape, they'll bring her faster than you can reach her.'

'Yeah, Doc. Chances are good that you won't even get close to the scene. You'll just be in the way.'

J.D. controlled his fury at the man's heartless remark. 'Katie could be critical and you're not anxious for someone to treat her?'

Hank looked taken aback. 'Of course I am, but Beth is right. You won't do her much good if you're caught in traffic and she's on her way here.'

Irritated by Hank's logical arguments, J.D. reached for the radio's microphone, depressed the transmit button and called for squad ten—Katie's squad—on their frequency.

No one answered.

He called for the other squad on the scene—squad twelve. They didn't answer either.

By now a small crowd of ER staff had gathered around the desk, but J.D. ignored them all as he continued to try and make contact.

Finally, a sheriff's deputy answered. 'Mercer, this is Unit 314. Squad twelve asked me to tell you to stand by.'

The implications became obvious to J.D.. Someone gasped aloud and others murmured among themselves as if they, too, understood why squad ten didn't respond to J.D.'s call and why squad twelve was too busy.

The minutes seemed to drag on. At long last a male voice came across the air waves, but his transmission was hard to hear because of static.

'Twenty…female… Possible head and…injuries. Unresponsive…'

Fear gripped J.D.'s heart at the familiar description.

'Medic alert…'

'Say again?' J.D. asked.

'Medic alert…asthma… BP is 90 over… Pulse is…'

J.D. stared at Beth in relief. Katie didn't have asthma. 'This must be the other passenger.'

'ETA…ten…'

'Squad twelve? What's the status of the EMT crew? Where's Katie?'

There was a brief pause before static came across the air waves again. 'Banged up…pretty bad…in ambulance… Over and out.'

'Banged up. Pretty bad.' The words bounced around in his head like berserk ping-pong balls.

'You heard him,' J.D. told the crowd. 'They're on their way.'

The group scattered to their posts. J.D. stood on the ambulance dock to wait. A ground-out cigarette butt lay in his line of vision, tossed carelessly onto the concrete instead of into the urn. Too bad he couldn't stand the smell of tobacco—he would have liked to have done something with his hands while the minutes dragged.

A gust of wind whipped around the corner. He hunched his shoulders and thrust his hands in his pockets. Out of the corner of his eye he watched Tristan and Beth approach.

'What a gloomy day,' she said. Then, shivering, she added, 'It's cold out here.'

'You don't have to keep me company.'

'And let you hog all the excitement?' Tristan joked. 'I don't think so.' He glanced at his watch. 'Don't you have a meeting to attend right now?'

'I'm not going.' J.D. enunciated each word carefully.

'I can cover for you. The board—'

'To hell with the board.' J.D. used his mildest—and deadliest—tone.

Tristan shrugged. 'I didn't expect you to leave. Just thought I'd ask.' His voice became serious. 'If Katie is in a bad way, I think you should let someone else take over.'

'Not a chance.'

'I thought you'd say that, too.'

A distant wail captured their attention. J.D. straightened, knowing he had about two minutes of waiting left.

The ambulance rolled to a stop in the street, then slowly backed up the driveway. Fearful over what he would find, and anxious to know one way or the other, he stood poised to spring. Before the driver had cut the engine J.D. had flung open the rear doors.

'Katie!' His shoulders sagged in relief.

Katie was standing between two stretchers. 'This one's first,' she ordered, pointing to the person on her left.

Lee grabbed hold of his end of the cot and pulled, revealing a completely immobilised victim.

J.D., however, had eyes for only one person and stated the obvious. 'You're OK.'

Katie readjusted the patient's oxygen mask. 'A little worse for the wear, but, yeah, I'm fine. One of the guys from twelve skinned his leg, diving out of the way, but Doug wasn't as lucky.'

Beth stood ready to receive the opposite end of the stretcher. Katie quickly ran down the list of information pertaining to her patient as J.D. focused on the details. He quickly checked the pupils, noting their unequal size.

'Get her inside to Dr Li,' he ordered once she'd finished her recitation. 'Get a CT scan, stat.'

Tristan helped Katie's driver—a fellow J.D. didn't recognise—pull the second victim from the vehicle. Doug groaned as they jostled his cot.

'Be careful,' Katie cautioned from her place inside the vehicle. 'I think his hip is broken.'

While Tristan and Beth pushed their gurney towards the door where Michael and Ashley were waiting, J.D. turned toward Katie, anxious to reassure himself of her safety.

Seeing she was about to hop out of the vehicle, he placed his hands on both sides of her ribcage and lifted her off the rear step. Showing a total lack of concern for any spectators—including Hank—he hugged her tightly.

'I love you,' he said before he kissed her.

She felt so good. But she wasn't his.

Reluctantly he released her, his eyes searching. 'Be happy, Katie.'

Her eyes glimmered with tears. 'J.D.,' she began, but got no further.

'Doctor?' Ashley called from the door. 'They're waiting for you.'

He cupped the side of her face, certain he wouldn't have the opportunity again—or the right—then rushed away.

'Your timing stinks, J.D.,' she called.

He paused to glance over his shoulder. 'I know,' he said, his voice laced with regret. Rushing inside, he felt her gaze drill into his back, but he couldn't look in her direction. It was too painful.

The next few hours were hectic, but he gratefully embraced the pace since it kept him focused on problems other than his own.

Between performing triage, treating victims with minor injuries and sending the worst cases to Surgery or Intensive Care, he reassured family members and spoke to the press.

J.D. had sent the last victim home by seven o'clock. The drama officially over, he was at a loss for something to do. He grabbed a handful of paper clips from the desk drawer and began straightening them.

At one time he'd thought he'd straighten his own life just as easily. The romantic evening he'd planned had seemed the perfect answer. Visions of Katie and a family of little Berkleys faded into one of only Daniel and himself.

Deep in his thoughts, he didn't notice Beth until she reached over the ledge and confiscated his rapidly dwindling pile of intact clips.

'You have a visitor. A VIP.'

He groaned, daunted by the idea of another reporter wanting an interview. 'Can't you talk to him? Or, better yet, refer them to Allan Yates. I'm busy.'

She eyed the pile of straight metal wires. 'Saving lives, too, I see.'

'Hey! I'm winding down.'

'Wind down later,' Beth said firmly. 'After you

go to the lounge.' As he opened his mouth to refuse, she added, 'Now.'

His shoulders slumped. He rubbed his face, feeling the start of a five-o'clock shadow. 'Is it that important?'

'Yes. Quit dawdling and go.'

'Before I forget, I won't need you to watch Daniel tonight.' Luckily, he hadn't told Daniel about the sleepover so he wouldn't dash his hopes.

'We'll talk about it later,' she said. 'You may change your mind. Now, hurry up before…'

He grew suspicious. 'Before what?'

'Before you either destroy all my paper clips or another catastrophe rolls through the door. Take your pick.'

'All right, all right. I'm going to request a private office, including a DO NOT DISTURB sign,' he grumbled, thinking of his recent visitors.

Beth grinned. 'Good idea.'

'If I'm not back in ten minutes, come and get me.'

'We'll see.'

'I mean it,' he insisted. 'Say I have a patient or a meeting—I don't care. Just come and get me.'

She heaved a great sigh. 'If you really want me to…'

'I really want you to,' he said firmly. A few minutes later he pasted a smile on his face before he pushed open the door to the lounge. 'I'm Dr Berkley,' he said. 'You asked to—'

Katie stepped into his line of vision.

'See me?' he finished, shaken by her presence.

'I certainly did,' she said.

Beth's comments suddenly made sense. He raised one eyebrow. 'Does Beth know you're here?'

'She sent you, didn't she?'

'Yes, but I didn't know who was waiting.'

Katie paused. 'Would you have come if you'd known?'

He leaned against the counter and dug his hands in his pockets. Although he wanted to hold her in the worst way, she was here for a reason and until he knew what it was he'd better keep his hands to himself.

'I'm not sure,' he said.

Her smile was tremulous. 'At least you're honest. Which is more than I can say for myself.'

He raised an eyebrow. 'Oh?'

'Before I explain, I heard you wanted to find me when you thought I might have been hit by the run-away car.'

Wondering where she was leading, he nodded.

'You would have lost your job for sure,' she told him.

His gaze didn't waver as it met hers. 'I know. Mercer isn't the only place to work.'

'You really would have done that? For me?' She sounded amazed.

He gave her a simple answer. 'Yes.'

'Did you mean what you said outside?'

'Every word.'

She heaved a great sigh before she began, 'I told you that I didn't want to meet this mystery fellow you had lined up.'

He didn't need a reminder. 'Yeah. Because there's someone else.'

She fingered her belt buckle. 'Two people, actually, but I was never brave enough to tell you who they were.'

Two men?

'I should have spoken out before this finding a wife business got out of hand, but I couldn't. I knew you weren't ready to hear that I loved you. And Daniel.'

All thoughts of Hank flew out of his mind. He straightened. 'Is this past tense?'

'Past, present and future.'

The stormclouds in his mood blew away, leaving only sunny skies. 'Oh, Katie.'

Tears glimmered in her eyes. 'I thought I'd never hear you say those three magical words.'

He held out his arms and she walked into his embrace. 'At first, I didn't recognise my feelings for what they were because they grew so naturally,' he confessed, inhaling the sweet scent of her hair.

'It worked that way for me, too. I felt so sorry for you in the beginning. You'd lost Ellen, had a tiny baby and were adjusting to a new job. I wanted to help. After a while my sentiments changed and I knew I had to be patient. It was hard, pretending to be friends when I wanted more.

'It was even more difficult to play hard to get when you first suggested marriage,' she finished ruefully. 'I wanted to say yes, but I wanted you to ask for the right reasons. Convenience wasn't one of them.'

It all made sense. J.D. pulled away slightly. 'I wasn't supposed to like those women you set me up with, was I?'

She giggled. 'No.'

He ran his fingers through her long tresses. 'And this was intended to get my attention.'

'You had to get over Ellen,' she said simply. 'I

thought we had a chance, until you asked me to help you find a suitable wife. Then I had to do *something* to get you to notice me.'

'I did.' He paused. 'Once I realised what you truly wanted and needed, I planned tonight as an evening to remember.'

Her eyebrows came together. 'I don't understand.'

'The man you were going to meet tonight was…me.'

'You?'

He gave her a lopsided grin. 'Yes. I had it all organised. Dinner by candlelight, wine, soft music— the works. I'd even arranged for Daniel to spend the night at Beth's. I don't mind telling you the bad moments I've had since you told me you'd found someone else.'

She rubbed the placket of his scrub shirt. 'I'm sorry for ruining your evening, although I must admit that Rose caused me a lot of bad moments too. She seemed tailor-made to the points on your list.'

Tucking his finger under her chin, J.D. lifted her head until her gaze met his. '*You* are the one who's made-to-order, Katie Alexander. I rewrote my list with you in mind. No one else.'

Katie's eyes widened in surprise. 'You did?'

'Yup. I wondered when you'd figure it out.'

Her voice sounded shocked and amazed. 'The qualities you listed… I tried to make myself into them, but—'

'You didn't have to because they were written with you in mind, including your freckles.' He touched the bridge of her nose.

'But I'm not athletic,' she protested. 'Or gorgeous, or sexy, or any of the things you asked for.'

'You are to me,' he assured her. 'Each and every one of them.'

'Rose seemed to fit far better than I did.'

'No, she didn't. On the other hand, I had the same problem with *your* list. I never thought of myself as a jealous man but when Hank came on the scene I was green with envy.'

'But why? I told you we didn't generate any sparks. After being with you, I couldn't possibly marry a man without any fire.'

'Too bad I cancelled my romantic dinner for two,' he mourned.

Katie gave him a flirtatious look as she flung her arms around his neck. 'It's OK. We're going to be too busy to eat, anyway.'

Hope—and love—stirred in his chest. 'I hope that's a promise.'

She answered him with a kiss. The embers within him suddenly burst into flames. The low sound coming from her throat was as stirring as the actual feel of her body pressed against his.

The drone of the switchboard operator's voice, announcing the end of visiting hours, brought him to earth.

'I told Beth she didn't have to take Daniel home tonight after all. She said I might change my mind.'

Katie's heavy-lidded eyes reflected his desire. 'Have you?'

J.D.'s lopsided grin came slow and easy. 'Do you really have to ask?'

J.D. walked into his house after his shift had ended, pleased to be home. Daniel's giggle and Katie's laughter filled the air as always, but during the past week the sound had been more special than ever because it marked an overdue change in each of their lives.

He peeked into the bathroom and found Katie towelling off his son, who bore a remarkable resemblance to a drowned rat.

'Daddy's home!'

'Run and get dressed,' she told Daniel. While he scurried toward his room to obey, Katie stood and greeted J.D. with her sunny smile. 'How did the meeting go? I've been dying to hear.'

'It's a long story,' he began.

'Start talking,' she ordered as she tried to wring the excess water out of her purple sweatshirt.

He faked a sigh. 'No respect. Here I'm getting more responsibility and my own fiancée orders me around.'

She jumped to her feet, squealing with delight as she rushed into his outstretched arms. 'They approved your project! Oh, J.D. How wonderful!' Her smile dimmed slightly. 'What about the policy issue?'

'Apparently Mr Pollard's family wrote a letter to the newspaper editor, praising my heroic efforts to save his life. Considering all the good publicity, the board didn't feel it was in anyone's best interests to censure me.'

'It isn't in *their* best interests, you mean,' she said tartly. 'The public outcry would be phenomenal.'

He smiled at her loyalty. 'Regardless of their excuse, everything worked out and that's the main thing.'

Daniel rushed in, wearing a pair of striped flannel

pyjamas, and tugged on J.D.'s hand. 'I've had my bath, Daddy. Is it time?'

'Time for what?' Katie asked.

'It's Daddy's and my secret,' Daniel said importantly before he yanked on J.D.'s fingers again. 'So, Daddy? Is it time?'

J.D. smiled. 'Yes, it's time.' At this news, Daniel scurried away.

Katie's eyes were bright with interest. 'What's going on?'

'We have something to give you,' J.D. said, leading her into the living room. 'So have a seat.'

Katie obeyed and Daniel returned with his hands behind his back. 'Close your eyes and hold out your hand,' he directed.

J.D. smiled at the command in his son's voice.

'Must be something special,' she answered, obeying.

Daniel handed J.D. the box. 'Open it for her, Daddy.'

J.D. raised the lid of a small jeweller's case and placed it on Katie's palm while Daniel fidgeted nearby.

'You can look now,' he said, his childish voice high with excitement.

Katie's eyelids shot open and she gasped at the sight of the custom-designed diamond ring. 'Oh, my goodness. It's beautiful.'

Daniel jumped onto the sofa beside her. 'Daddy and I had 'em make it special. Just for you.'

Katie's eyes sparkled as she looked at J.D. 'You did?'

J.D. smiled. 'It seemed appropriate.'

Tears came to her eyes as she understood the significance. A made-to-order ring for his made-to-order bride.

MILLS & BOON®

*Makes
any time
special*

Copyright © Harlequin Enterprises I Limited 1997
All rights reserved

**Enjoy a romantic novel from
Mills & Boon®**

Presents...™ *Enchanted*™ TEMPTATION.

Historical Romance™ ✓**MEDICAL
ROMANCE**™

MILLS & BOON®

MEDICAL ROMANCE™

THE COURAGE TO SAY YES by Lilian Darcy
Southshore #2 of 4

Paediatric surgeon Angus Ferguson had seen Caitlin Gray's fiancé, Scott, with another woman. Could he persuade her to see through Scott and look favourably on himself?

DOCTORS IN CONFLICT by Drusilla Douglas

The attraction between Catriona MacFarlane, the new Medical Registrar, and Michael Preston, orthopaedic surgeon, was *definitely* mutual, but when they both had such set ideas, how would they learn to compromise?

THE PERFECT TREATMENT by Rebecca Lang

Dr Abby Gibson was thrilled to discover she would be working with highly esteemed Dr Blake Contini. Although it was obvious from his warm smiling manner that Blake liked her, *something* was stopping him offering more than friendship...

PERFECT TIMING by Alison Roberts
The dawn of a new age...

Surgeon Jack Armstrong and nurse Amanda Morrison clashed horribly. It was their mutual delight in an elderly patient who would be one hundred years old on the first day of the new Millennium that brought them closer...

Available from 3rd December 1999

Available at most branches of WH Smith, Tesco, Martins, Borders, Easons, Volume One/James Thin and most good paperback bookshops

MILLS & BOON®

MEDICAL
ROMANCE™

NEW

**From
Lilian Darcy**

SOUTHSHORE

Medicine and Marriage
Southshore has it all.

Look out for no.2 in the quartet

The Courage to Say Yes

Available 3rd December

*Available at most branches of WH Smith, Tesco,
Martins, Borders, Easons, Volume One/James Thin
and most good paperback bookshops*

MILLENNIUM

Celebrate the Millennium with your favourite romance authors. With so many to choose from, there's a Millennium story for everyone!

Presents...™

> **Morgan's Child**
> **Anne Mather**
> On sale 3rd December 1999

Enchanted™

> **Bride 2000**
> **Trisha David**
> On sale 3rd December 1999

TEMPTATION®

> **Once a Hero**
> **Kate Hoffmann**
> On sale 3rd December 1999

> **Always a Hero**
> **Kate Hoffmann**
> On sale 7th January 2000

MEDICAL ROMANCE™

> **Perfect Timing**
> **Alison Roberts**
> On sale 3rd December 1999

MILLS & BOON®

Makes any time special™

MILLS & BOON®

MISTLETOE *Magic*

Three favourite Enchanted™ authors
bring you romance at Christmas.

Three stories in one volume:

A Christmas Romance
BETTY NEELS

Outback Christmas
MARGARET WAY

Sarah's First Christmas
REBECCA WINTERS

Published 19th November 1999

*Available at most branches of WH Smith, Tesco,
Martins, Borders, Easons, Volume One/James Thin
and most good paperback bookshops*

2 Books
and a surprise gift!

We would like to take this opportunity to thank you for reading this Mills & Boon® book by offering you the chance to take TWO more specially selected titles from the Medical Romance™ series absolutely FREE! We're also making this offer to introduce you to the benefits of the Reader Service™—

- ★ FREE home delivery
- ★ FREE gifts and competitions
- ★ FREE monthly Newsletter
- ★ Books available before they're in the shops
- ★ Exclusive Reader Service discounts

Accepting these FREE books and gift places you under no obligation to buy; you may cancel at any time, even after receiving your free shipment. Simply complete your details below and return the entire page to the address below. *You don't even need a stamp!*

YES! Please send me 2 free Medical Romance books and a surprise gift. I understand that unless you hear from me, I will receive 4 superb new titles every month for just £2.40 each, postage and packing free. I am under no obligation to purchase any books and may cancel my subscription at any time. The free books and gift will be mine to keep in any case.

M9EB

Ms/Mrs/Miss/Mr ....Initials...

BLOCK CAPITALS PLEASE

Surname..

Address...

....

....Postcode ....

Send this whole page to:
UK: The Reader Service, FREEPOST CN81, Croydon, CR9 3WZ
EIRE: The Reader Service, PO Box 4546, Kilcock, County Kildare (stamp required)

Offer not valid to current Reader Service subscribers to this series. We reserve the right to refuse an application and applicants must be aged 18 years or over. Only one application per household. Terms and prices subject to change without notice. Offer expires 31st May 2000. As a result of this application, you may receive further offers from Harlequin Mills & Boon Limited and other carefully selected companies. If you would prefer not to share in this opportunity please write to The Data Manager at the address above.

Mills & Boon is a registered trademark owned by Harlequin Mills & Boon Limited.
Medical Romance is being used as a trademark.

GIRL *in the* MIRROR
MARY ALICE MONROE

Charlotte Godowski and Charlotte Godfrey
are two sides to the same woman—a woman
who can trust no one with her secret. But
when fate forces Charlotte to deal with the
truth about her past, about the man she loves,
about her self—she discovers that only love
has the power to transform a scarred soul.

MIRA®   Available from 22nd October